THE
LOST
SONGS

NOVELS BY
CAROLINE B. COONEY

The Lost Songs
Three Black Swans
They Never Came Back
If the Witness Lied
Diamonds in the Shadow
A Friend at Midnight
Hit the Road
Code Orange
The Girl Who Invented Romance
Family Reunion
Goddess of Yesterday
The Ransom of Mercy Carter
Tune In Anytime
Burning Up
What Child Is This?
Driver's Ed
Twenty Pageants Later
Among Friends
The Time Travelers, Volumes I and II

The Janie Books

The Face on the Milk Carton
Whatever Happened to Janie?
The Voice on the Radio
What Janie Found

The Time Travel Quartet

Both Sides of Time
Out of Time
Prisoner of Time
For All Time

CAROLINE B. COONEY

THE
LOST
SONGS

DELACORTE PRESS

Text copyright © 2011 by Caroline B. Cooney
Jacket photograph copyright © 2011 by Ghida el Souki

All rights reserved. Published in the United States by Delacorte Press, an imprint of Random House Children's Books, a division of Random House, Inc., New York.

Delacorte Press is a registered trademark and the colophon is a trademark of Random House, Inc.

Visit us on the Web! www.randomhouse.com/teens
Educators and librarians, for a variety of teaching tools, visit us at www.randomhouse.com/teachers

Library of Congress Cataloging-in-Publication Data
Cooney, Caroline B.
  The lost songs / Caroline B. Cooney. — 1st ed.
    p. cm.
  Summary: In small-town Carolina, sixteen-year-old Lutie Painter treasures the "Laundry List" of songs written by her ancestor and does not want to share them, but ultimately they help her learn more about her absent mother and connect with fellow students Kelvin, Doria, and especially Train, a former friend.
  ISBN 978-0-385-73966-5 (hardcover) — ISBN 978-0-385-90800-9 (glb) — ISBN 978-0-375-89805-1 (ebook)
  [1. Interpersonal relations—Fiction. 2. Conduct of life—Fiction. 3. Folk songs, English—Fiction. 4. Mothers and daughters—Fiction. 5. African Americans—Fiction. 6. High schools—Fiction. 7. Schools—Fiction.]   I. Title.
  PZ7.C7834Los 2011   [Fic]—dc22   2010039975

The text of this book is set in 12-point Adobe Garamond.
Book design by Vikki Sheatsley
Printed in the United States of America
10 9 8 7 6 5 4 3 2 1
First Edition

Thursday
Morning
COURT HILL HIGH SCHOOL

Lutie endangers her life.

Doria stands alone.

Kelvin half notices.

Train finds a victim.

*A piece of American history floats
just out of reach.*

1

Lutie Painter had never skipped school before. Not once. Never faked being sick, never lied about where she was going. She had friends who averaged a day or even two days a week when they shrugged off school and did something else. Not Lutie.

But the dawn phone call from Saravette had gone through Lutie's heart like birdshot. Saravette used a telephone only if she needed something. It was never Lutie she called. Lutie was excited and frightened. In a minute, she was up and dressed, telling lies and racing out the door. She caught the city bus north instead of the school bus west.

Lutie's aunts would never have allowed her to do this. When her aunts were forced to refer to Saravette, their lips pinched and their voices tightened. A person on crack and crystal meth was not rational or safe. Her aunts rarely referred to Saravette as their sister.

Lutie had not stopped to think about clothing. She liked a different look every day of the week. Yesterday had been slinky: black and silver and armloads of bracelets. Today was pink: pink and white book bag on her back, little rose-puff rse with a ribbon shoulder strap, cute little pink sneakers and sweet cotton-candy-pink hoodie. She probably looked twelve. Did this make her more or less safe?

The bus route into the city was long and the bus driver did everything he could to shorten it. He was definitely a NASCAR fan. He stopped with neck-snapping lurches when somebody signaled from the curb, and then roared forward with such disregard for traffic that Lutie, also a race fan, had to close her eyes.

Lutie's grandmother had ridden this very bus to work six days a week. Imagine doing this twice a day all your life. Lutie studied her fellow riders. Anybody taking a bus must have the same daydream: to own a car. It required such patience to ride a bus. Why was patience a virtue? What was the good thing about patience? It was *im*patience that paid off. Impatient people got stuff done. Patient people were still standing there waiting.

She thought about Saravette, who didn't have virtues.

On the phone, Saravette's voice had been thready and weak, as if she were ill. But one sentence had been strong and sharp: "You have to know," said Saravette suddenly.

And when Saravette disconnected, Lutie did have to know. What, after all this time, did Saravette need to tell her?

The bus sped through remnants of farmland. In the last ten years, the population of the county had tripled. Every time you turned around, bulldozers had cleared another mile of woods. A minute later a network of paved roads crisscrossed the red dirt. An hour after that, two hundred new houses with identical landscaping were on the market. All those families needed stores and banks and fast food. Buildings leaped into place, as if they had been waiting in the wings like actors. The original village of Court Hill was hard to find, swallowed by this flood of housing and schools and churches and Walmarts.

themselves. There hadn't been many. MeeMaw's joys had been church, cooking, the front porch and, above all, Lutie.

The bus approached a swell of tall office buildings, and most of the remaining passengers got off. The strangers had been a comfort. Now Lutie's courage collapsed. So did the city. The buildings got lower and weaker. The sidewalks were cracked and the streets full of litter. Stores existed here and there, half of them boarded up or wrapped in crime tape.

It was difficult to tell if the parked cars were abandoned or if people actually drove those dented paintless hulks. There weren't many people. Even the grim city housing projects seemed empty. Maybe if you were the loitering type, you weren't up yet.

The only other passenger now was a skinny young man with an excess of tattoos. His eyes were closed and his head waved on its stalk, as if his neck were only a temporary connection to his body.

Lutie counted down the streets. Ninth. Eighth. Seventh. This is it, she thought. She raised her hand to touch the stop sensor, then panicked. Forget it. She couldn't get off here. She'd ride to the end of the route instead, safe inside the bus, pay the driver again, and take it all the way home.

And then she saw Saravette leaning against a telephone pole.

Lutie realized that she had not actually expected Saravette to be here. Saravette, who forgot everything or lied about it to start with, was not usually where she was supposed to be.

Lutie's lungs filled in little spurts, as if she were breathing in code. She signaled for a stop. The brakes on the bus squealed. Lutie tottered down the long empty aisle. The driver raised his eyebrows and nodded toward the neighborhood. "You know what you're doing?"

Lutie had no idea what she was doing.

The bus roared past sprawling malls, vast retirement vil-
lages and strings of town-house developments, each with its
pretend British name—Therrington and Land Brooke and
Churchill Meade. It stopped at medical centers and factories
and the campuses of corporate offices. Everything was tidy.
Each prim little tree had a careful donut of pine straw mulch.
The buildings and landscaping and charming low brick walls
were so similar that Lutie could not tell where she was.

Like my heart, she thought. I can't tell where it is either.

She never liked thinking about Saravette. She never liked
picturing Saravette.

It would take an hour to get to the far side of the city, so
Lutie slid her shoulders out of her book bag and riffled
through the contents, thinking she might use the hour fruit-
fully and master a few facts for chemistry. Lutie loved school.
Actually, everybody loved school, but most kids were sorry
that school had to go and include class. Lutie used to feel
sheepish for studying so much. This year, she was mostly in
AP and honors classes, though, and it was easier to learn when
the rest of the class liked learning too.

The bus was now on a boulevard, miles of island dividers
planted with a single row of crape myrtle trees and beds of
pansies eternally smiling at traffic. Somewhere in this neighborhood, Lutie's grandmother had kept house for a family she
was very fond of. They'd paid MeeMaw better than most
housekeepers were paid. They hadn't paid into Social Security,
because they never thought of it, and MeeMaw had never
thought of it either, and in fact had never paid taxes, because
she was vague on how that was supposed to happen. When the
couple moved away to be closer to their grandchildren,
MeeMaw had nothing. Lutie's aunts had arranged Supple-
mental Security Income, which provided a few hundred dollars a month, and then they had paid the rest of the bills

"This is not a good place," said the driver, which was certainly true.

Lutie pointed at Saravette. "She's waiting for me."

The driver took in the sight of Saravette. Thirty years old, looked eighty. Sunken cheeks from lost teeth. Tattoos and piercings no longer brave and sassy, but pitiful. Wearing two sweaters on an already hot morning. Both dirty.

My mother, thought Lutie.

Impossible. The wreck on the sidewalk could not be related to her.

"You got a cell phone?" said the driver.

"Yes, sir."

"You worried, you call nine-one-one. But remember, around here, they're slow."

Lutie would have expected that around here, the police would be fast. Maybe on this block, the police had surrendered.

Carefully, as if the steps were made of glass, Lutie got off the bus. Every other time, the instant his passenger's foot hit the pavement, the driver's foot hit the accelerator. This time he waited and kept the door open. Lutie loved him for that. She forced herself to walk over to Saravette, who gave her a light smelly hug. Lutie cringed.

Saravette led the way to a side street, and then the bus did leave, spewing a puff of diesel thick enough for breakfast. Saravette was talking, but Lutie could not follow the sense of it. The mumbled words did not connect.

They went into a scary coffee shop, where they sat among scary people. Lutie could not touch her mug. Somebody else's fingerprints were greasily pasted on the china. The air-conditioning in the sad little room barely swirled the air. The grease from a million fried meals settled on her skin.

In a metal chair with a torn vinyl back, Saravette rocked herself. She never stopped talking, but it was just stuff, as if she

7

were reading miscellaneous lines from pieces of paper blowing in the street.

Lutie tried to think of something to say, some little story to tell about what she was doing these days, but she did not know where to start. Once upon a time, Saravette had led Lutie's life. How did you get here from there? Lutie wanted to scream at her. Why didn't you just go home again? What keeps you in this horrible place?

Saravette lit a cigarette. The smoke in her lungs seemed to calm her. The next sentence was rational. "You still going to Miss Veola's church?"

Miss Veola was their pastor. She all but stalked the teenagers in her congregation, checking on their homework, their morals and their grammar. "Yes," said Lutie, relieved to be making a contribution to the conversation.

"She still comes to find me sometimes," said Saravette.

"I know."

"I'm one of her lost ones," said Saravette proudly. "I surely am. Miss Veola's still preaching at me. There's a lot to preach about too. By now," said Saravette, laughing, "I've broken all the commandments."

Lutie's head hummed like the struggling window unit while Saravette rocked and smiled. "You've broken *all* the commandments?" whispered Lutie. One in the middle of the list, say? Thou shalt not kill?

Saravette laughed and nodded and rocked.

She's using the Ten Commandments as a metaphor, Lutie told herself, as if the diner were honors English class and the teacher were discussing literature. Saravette has not broken *all* the commandments. She did not kill anybody. This is just another fib. Saravette's probably forgotten what the Ten Commandments even are.

8

Saravette put out her cigarette and immediately lit it again. For the first time, her eyes met Lutie's and stayed focused. "You have to know something," she said quietly. It was not the voice of a crazy person to a stranger. It was the voice of a mother to her daughter.

Panic filled Lutie Painter. It was bad enough to know that this sad smelly sack of failed person was her mother. But whatever had made Saravette telephone Lutie instead of the aunts and the pastor who continually and grimly came to Saravette's rescue was probably something Lutie *didn't* want to know.

Saravette had a coughing fit. Her skin took on a gray tinge as the cough choked its way out of her throat. The other customers glared, as if they'd be perfectly willing to choke Saravette themselves for making such a racket. Lutie gripped her purse hard, trying to calm her trembling fingers. This was not a place where people should see you break down.

When the cough ended, Saravette looked like a ghost of herself. The two of them sat in silence. Saravette lit another cigarette and continued to rock and smile.

Lutie imagined Saravette rocking and smoking and smiling as she broke each commandment. Swear? Check.

Steal? Check.

Kill? Check.

"I skipped school," Lutie said loudly. "What did you need to tell me? Why did you beg me to come?"

Saravette turned away. She still had a beautiful profile. She stopped breathing, whether to suppress a coughing fit or to steel herself to talk, Lutie did not know.

"Give me a minute," whispered Saravette. "Then I'll be ready." She signaled one of the scary guys at the counter. The man—who looked hardly older than Lutie—hooked his thumbs in his sweatpants and sauntered over, smirking.

She's going to buy drugs, thought Lutie. Right now. With me sitting here.

Saravette's breathing become shallow and quick. Her eyes lit up. The man-boy sat down at the table with them. One hundred percent of Saravette's attention was on him.

She's already forgotten what she said, thought Lutie. What's murder, after all? Just one in a list of ten. Whatever.

Lutie was afraid to get up from the table, afraid to walk out of the coffee shop, let alone walk back to the bus stop. She picked up the little piece of paper on which their tab was scribbled and went over to the woman at the register. The woman was big and heavy, with breasts the size of water-melons. Lutie couldn't imagine balancing all that. She opened her wallet. Her fingers felt stiff.

The woman took the money with a sort of fury and glared at Lutie. "How you getting home, girl?"

"Bus," whispered Lutie.

"I'm going with you." The woman shifted her glare to the prep cook, who shrugged, which maybe meant that he would take over the register and maybe meant that he couldn't care less whether anybody ran the register at all.

The woman marched Lutie out of the coffee shop. Saravette did not call to her and Lutie did not say good-bye. They walked past people Lutie did not want to know better, crossed the main street in the middle of the block and stood under the little sign for the bus stop.

The bus appeared almost immediately, which was a good thing. Lutie's knees were shaking and her heart was falling out. Her mother might be a murderer.

"Thank you," whispered Lutie.

"Don't cry, honey," said the woman. "And don't come back."

2

The bus ride home seemed quicker. Lutie got off at her grandmother's old stop, although she could have ridden farther. The bus would finish its route across from Lutie's high school and then circle behind the post office and head back uptown.

Lutie stood by the road for a while, as if waiting for a transfer, or else brain cells. Then she crossed the street.

It had been a hot summer and it was a hot autumn. The air was thick and damp. Lutie did not enter Chalk, but crossed a little bridge over Peter Creek, turned up a gravel driveway and approached a little wood house with a little wood porch. When MeeMaw was alive, she used to line the porch with geraniums in coffee cans, a symphony of bright blue containers and fire-engine-red flowers. MeeMaw had died when Lutie was twelve and Lutie missed her every day.

Lutie owned the house now, but it was rented out. Sometimes Lutie dreamed of living in the tiny home where she had grown up. She would put in central air and granite countertops. She would sit on the porch, like MeeMaw, and soak up the sun.

But more often, Lutie wanted her ticket out. She wanted to go to Atlanta or Austin or Nashville. Maybe become a scientist and show the world she deserved her placement in honors chemistry. Or maybe teach kindergarten, because she adored little kids, who were all so beautiful. Sometimes she wanted to be a nomad and travel forever, just her and a change of clothing, her passport and a cell phone.

Houses without a garage could not deceive you. No car in the driveway meant nobody was home. Lutie could trespass.

She sat on the bottom step, knees close to her chin, and felt MeeMaw standing behind her in the doorway, wiping her hands on her apron and saying that dinner was ready. Lutie smothered a sob. MeeMaw, what if somebody isn't alive anymore because of Saravette? Do I just go on to school? Take a quiz and laugh with my friends? Brush my teeth tonight and go to bed? Say to myself, Oh well, stuff happens?

MeeMaw had gotten all her answers from the Lord. She would have walked out on the grass—a meadow, actually, mowed occasionally, full of flowers and bees and butterflies. MeeMaw could get seriously annoyed with God. She used to stand in the middle of the field where he could see her better, peer into the sky and let him know his shortcomings.

"What am I supposed to do?" MeeMaw would holler.

Lutie wasn't counting on the Lord. If he planned to guide somebody's steps, he should have guided Saravette's.

She remembered how MeeMaw would stride into the sun. Throw her head back. Take that extraordinary deep breath to fill those amazing lungs. Turn both hands up, as if holding the song on her two palms, offering it to heaven.

Lutie even knew what MeeMaw would have sung. So Lutie too walked into the view of the Lord, took her own deep breath and looked up to see if she could spot him. There were a hawk floating and a cloud drifting.

12

It was different singing outdoors than it was in the high school music room or the church choir loft. Her voice was a living thing, like any living thing; like the mockingbirds and the chattering flow of Peter Creek. She knew that her voice floated over all of Chalk. The whole neighborhood would know that Lutie Painter had skipped school and was over at her MeeMaw's, singing her heart out.

Nobody would tell. Chalk was a neighborhood where you never ratted on anybody for anything.

Lutie sang.

"Don't see no sign of you.
This ain't so fine of you,
Leaving me here all alone.

"Don't see no sign of you.
This ain't so fine of you,
Sitting high on your throne.

"We your children or not, God?
You're all we've got, God.
And you're leaving us here all alone."

The melody shouted through the clouds, phrases tumbling over each other, repeating and doubling back. The Lord could not miss the message.

After MeeMaw would sing this one, she used to add a disclaimer. "Of course he never leaves our side, honey," she'd say to Lutie, "and we are always his through the grace of Jesus Christ. Now do your homework, study hard and make me proud."

There was but one way to make her grandmother proud. Go to school.

Lutie did not want to sit in class with kids whose mothers were not murderers. Which presumably was everybody. What if people found out? The news of having a murderer for a mother would ooze like an oil spill. Saravette would seep into Lutie's life and taint everything.

Lutie prayed that Saravette—who had chosen all these years to stay away—would keep on staying away.

Well, that was a sick little prayer, she thought. God, keep my mother out of sight.

Now she needed an excuse for being so late to school. "I didn't feel good," she practiced, "but now I do."

Who could argue with that?

She didn't usually admit it when she felt bad, because Aunt Tamika and Aunt Grace had grim responses to claims of being sick. They would insist that she eat chicken noodle soup. Lutie hated soup. Especially canned soup. Especially canned chicken soup. And if she ended up with Miss Veola instead of an aunt because both her aunts were at work, the pastor would sit by Lutie's bed and pray.

Lutie decided not to go into the high school by the front door, where the office kept an eye on things and where she would have to produce her excuse. She would enter by the stage door, which was always propped open. She'd be early for chorus, but Mr. Gregg would not wonder why. It never occurred to him that anybody might have a life other than music. He'd assign her to rearrange chairs or something, and ask her to come this early every day.

The music room was enormous. Bands, orchestra, choruses, theory and composition classes—all had to share. A forest of black music stands, tympani under their tents and boxes of infrequently used percussion instruments crowded up against the grand piano. Mr. Gregg was a demanding choral conductor. When rehearsal began, Lutie would be able to lose herself in the music and forget Saravette. *I've broken all the commandments.* (Laughter. Pride.)

Mr. Gregg was a big overweight guy, shirt untucked, tie askew, and had a big overweight office to match. Sheet music and CDs and programs and books spilled out of cabinets and drawers, teetered in piles on the floor and were stacked so high on the visitor's chair that it looked as if a tall square person were sitting there. The office's two interior walls were used as a bulletin board. Mr. Gregg put stuff up but never took stuff down, so the bulletin board had become a dusty art project. The glass outer walls were so smeared with fingerprints they were barely see-through.

"Lutie!" yelled Mr. Gregg, beaming.

"Good morning, Mr. Gregg."

Mr. Gregg had no capacity for small talk. He would never dream of asking how you were, because you might tell him, which would waste valuable music time.

"This is great, Lutie!" he cried. "I asked the office to find you, but could they pull it off? No. Buncha losers up there. Well, we have only ten minutes, but that could be enough! Let's get to work."

Mr. Gregg had asked the office to find her?

Imperfect. Highly imperfect.

They would have telephoned one or all of her homes. She would be in trouble in three locations. But maybe it was for the best. Maybe she ought to tell Aunt Grace and Aunt Tamika and Miss Veola what Saravette had said. But what if they didn't brush off the possibility that Saravette was a murderer? What if they confirmed it?

Lutie thought of the cigarette in Saravette's fingers. What else had those fingers held? Murder was a do-it-yourself

15

activity. There had to be a technique and a tool. The murderer lifted the knife or the gun and then used it. On another person.

"Lutie," shouted Mr. Gregg, for whom life was a full-volume event, "I want you to meet Professor Martin Durham!"

She had not noticed that there was another adult present. Mr. Gregg hated visitors. They got in his way, had different standards, took up good teaching time and were bound to demand paperwork.

The professor was smaller than Mr. Gregg, and very dark. He had narrow features and an egg-bald head. He wore a gray suit with a gleaming vest, and a tie striped in blue, orange and red, like a beachfront awning. He was adorable in a middle-aged way. Almost bouncing, he extended his hand. "I am *so* delighted to meet you! This is *such* a privilege." He took Lutie's hand and pumped it, beaming.

Lutie took refuge in Southern courtesy, so helpful when stalling. "Sir," she said, trying to get her bearings.

"Professor Durham," explained Mr. Gregg, "used to be the director of the Center for African American Music at the University of South Carolina. He now has his own gospel recording company in Nashville and manages the American Music History department of the museum."

"And I'm here, of course," said Professor Durham, "because of your wonderful heritage."

Lutie thought of her heritage sitting in a filthy diner buying drugs.

"He means your grandmother's singing," said Mr. Gregg. "Whenever I'm at a music teachers' convention or leading a choral directors' workshop, somebody is bound to ask, 'Don't you teach in Court Hill? Isn't that where the lost songs are?' Well, I mean, of course I had *heard* of the lost songs, but I didn't

16

make the connection! Lutie! It's you! Sitting in my own soprano section all this time!"

Lutie stilled her face. It was an old skill, drawn from generations of faces that chose not to participate. She knew how to look dumb as a stump. It frightened her, how easily that ability surfaced and how well it stuck.

"Lutie has a beautiful, beautiful voice," Mr. Gregg told the professor. "Amazing range and depth. Lutie, sing one of those folk songs for us, okay?"

They were not folk songs. Folk music was public. Folk songs belonged to "folk," whoever they were. The lost songs, however, were Lutie's and Lutie's alone. "Sir?" she said vaguely.

Mr. Gregg could not believe that Lutie was not bursting into song. "Lutie, those songs have never been written down! They've never been recorded!" He shook his head in disbelief. "Imagine that! Songs composed by descendants of slaves—I mean, that's heavy. The crazy nickname put me off, you know? The Laundry List? Why would you refer to your compositions like that? That's why I didn't pay much attention to the story. But Lutie, Professor Durham has proved that this collection resides with a family named Painter. Lutie! You are a Painter."

The professor was smiling and nodding, the way Saravette had. "I've tracked you down, Miz Painter," he said, "and I'm a happy man."

Tracked her down? It sounded like the kind of thing you bought insurance against, to prevent strangers from stealing your identity. "Lots of Painters," said Lutie, staying neutral.

"And you probably know them all. You can get the lost songs for us," said Mr. Gregg.

The songs were *not* lost. They were privately held.

Lutie employed three types of speech. For school, she used what she thought of as weather-forecaster English: unaccented speech with carefully arranged sentences. Out of school, she slid into the local warm-honey drawl. "Isn't it?" became "idn't it" and "can" became "kin." She could also speak Chalk, the dialect of the neighborhood where MeeMaw had brought up her family. When Lutie spoke Chalk, she might omit the verb and the plural, stretch the vowels, drop a consonant here, add one there. "That costs five dollars" became "Tha' fi' dollah." And of course Miss Veola, her pastor, used a fourth language that came from decades of reading the King James Version of the Bible out loud: verses so rhythmic and lyrical, they were music on their own. Her speech was full of verses from Psalms and Isaiah and the punch lines of parables.

Lutie distanced herself with her Chalk voice. "Mr. Gregg," she said. *Mis-tah Grayg.* "I'm taking five classes this year?" *Fi' class this yeah?* "Honors chemistry is one of them?" *Wun a thim?* "I do not have time to chase rumors."

"It's no rumor," said the professor. "But Mr. Gregg is a little off track. The composer was not your grandmother, of course, but your great-great-grandmother, Mabel Painter. I've dreamed for years that I would finally find the Laundry List. And Miss Lutie, here you are!"

Both men were right. MeeMaw's grandmother *had* written the songs. Well, not written them, exactly, since they had never been put on paper. But songed them up herself. MeeMaw, Mabel's granddaughter, changed the songs here and there, adding verses and softening edges, because she felt they were rough on God. (Miss Veola snorted. "God can take it," said the pastor.)

MeeMaw had dealt with researchers over the years. University people, preachers, agents, history buffs, local musicians. Give me the songs, they said. As if MeeMaw ran a little corner grocery and would be happy to trot down the aisle, pluck one of her songs off a shelf and hand it over for a quarter.

18

MeeMaw always sent them away empty.

"Some people inherit land," she used to tell Lutie. "Or silver spoons or oil wells. You and me, we inherited songs. They're my grandma's shouts to God. Her prayers got answered too late for her. Instead, her prayers were answered for you, Lutie. You'll have the world she wanted. It's her prayers gave you this life. God was slow, I don't know why he was slow, but here you are, in the world *my* grandma told God to give you. You hold Mabel Painter's songs tight, baby girl. You put them in your heart and you keep them there."

For Lutie, it was the eleventh commandment. *You hold Mabel Painter's songs tight, baby girl. You put them in your heart and you keep them there.*

"Miss Lutie, did your grandmother Eunice ever talk about the songs?" asked the professor.

Who would talk about music when she could sing it? "Y'all have the right Painter?" asked Lutie, her drawl so thick even a Southerner could get lost in it. "Painters all over Ireland County."

"I did the genealogy," explained the professor. "Mabel Painter had a son, Isaac. Isaac Painter married Louene Moore. Their daughter Eunice was your grandmother. Now, Miss Eunice, she married a distant cousin, also named Painter, so she became Eunice Painter Painter, and her third baby was Saravette Painter, and y'all are Miss Saravette's little girl, Lutie."

If only, thought Lutie. If only there were some lovely young woman named Miss Saravette and her little girl, Lutie.

"Lutie, sing one for me?" begged the professor.

So far he had tried "Miz Painter," and "Miss Lutie," and now just "Lutie" in his attempt to make friends. "You see," he told her, "South Carolina was a portal for African and Caribbean slaves, and they brought extraordinary music traditions. Much has been lost forever, and the idea that something still exists is exciting! But of course, nobody's heard the songs, so I can't make any identification."

Nobody had heard the songs? What a riot. If the professor were to drive into Chalk right now, he'd find plenty of people who had just heard Lutie sing one, her voice filtering through the trees and over Peter Creek.

Lutie was attracted to enthusiasm. She liked the professor. But she said, "I think the Laundry List is just a story."

"A really good story," he said softly, "corroborated by many a source. A woman who spent her life taking in laundry for white folks, and whose spirituals were legendary. I think of the Laundry List as a treasure belonging to the world, Lutie. Music composed by a woman whose parents were probably slaves. Her songs alive by a thread. And the thread is *you*. To-gether we can return those songs to the world. Mabel Painter's songs," he added, as if reciting the name of a saint.

Mabel Painter might have been a saint, but if so, she'd been a very irritable one. Mabel Painter had ironed. She had ironed without air-conditioning in the hot Carolina weather. Without an electric fan. Without electricity, for that matter. And all day long, she sang.

There was even an ironing song, full of toil and despera-tion. Whenever Lutie sang the ironing song, it caught her by the soul and dragged her back to grim times and grimmer futures. She wondered what Mabel Painter would have thought of Saravette, who went and chose grim times when she could have had a good life.

"Miss Lutie, I'm hoping today after school will work for you. Can we talk a little more and maybe record a few of the songs?" asked the professor.

Steal them is what you actually mean, Lutie thought.

She considered changing her expression to sullen, which always infuriated adults. But she wanted the professor to forget about her. So she stayed polite and confused.

"If you haven't come across the songs, Lutie," said Mr. Gregg, "maybe another member of the family or somebody from an older generation knows them. Give me the email addresses of your grandparents. Or great-aunts. Elderly cousins."

"That old? Using a computer? I don't *think* so."

"Cell phones, then. Everybody uses a cell. Give everybody a call."

Lutie shook her head. "I don't think I can help," she said, as if it grieved her. She joined the crush of kids coming in for chorus and made her way up the risers to the top row of sopranos. She looked carefully at the chair before she sat, as if otherwise she would fall through it, going down, down, down to where Saravette was.

That professor had crawled around in her family history. If Lutie was no help, he'd easily find Aunt Grace and Aunt Tamika. They were not musical, had never cared about the songs and had largely discarded church and God anyway. They probably couldn't supply the songs themselves.

But Saravette had once known them all. Saravette, who would do anything for a dollar.

Few people knew about Saravette. Chalk looked much as it had for decades, but there was transience. Saravette had been gone a long time. Probably nobody there could tell Professor Durham how to locate her. He certainly wouldn't find Saravette using online sources: she was part of the population whose computer use was limited to stealing one, then selling it.

If Professor Durham did find Saravette, what might she say? "I broke all the commandments." (Laughter. Pride.)

Maybe he had already reached her. Maybe *that* was what Saravette had telephoned about.

No. If the professor had met Saravette, he would not have spoken lightly about her.

A terrible thought chiseled Lutie's heart, cutting a permanent place for itself. *I broke all the commandments.* What if that had just happened? What if that was what Saravette had wanted Lutie to know? "I did it, Lutie! I had only broken nine commandments, but I finally finished the list. Broke the last one last night. Killed a person."

Who?

Who had Saravette Painter killed?

3

"All rise!" shouted Mr. Gregg, and the singers reluctantly rose from the seats they had just taken. Mr. Gregg made them stand for warm-ups. Nobody liked standing. Nobody liked warm-up exercises either. Five long tedious minutes passed until Mr. Gregg bellowed, "Sit!" and the students dropped heavily into their chairs.

Kelvin dropped the most heavily.

The chorus chairs were arranged in a semicircle on three tiers. Kelvin was the outside baritone in the second row, facing the sopranos. Kelvin adored girls. There were ten in chorus alone whom he especially admired. Actually, he admired all girls for one reason or another—their being girls was enough—but in this room, maybe in any room, Lutie came first.

Lutie danced even when she was sitting. Other girls talked nonstop or stared at their fingernails or played with their hair, but Lutie put every molecule of energy into everything she did. Kelvin thought Lutie could become a choreographer or a surgeon. His parents would say to him, "Could you spend one minute thinking about what *you* want to be?"

But Kelvin was already what he wanted to be: welcome anywhere. He had no best friend. He had no group. It seemed to him that best friends lost out on other wonderful friends, and tight groups got bogged down in status. But a friend to all, like Kelvin, was room temperature. He was never too hot or too cold. He was always just right.

Kelvin wouldn't have minded being terrific at something, but his ambition was also room temperature. He didn't even expend effort watching television, and couldn't be bothered to locate the remote or rouse himself to go to the kitchen for a snack. When Kelvin found a place to sprawl, he liked to stay for a while and take in the scenery.

Chorus was outstanding in its scenery.

He wondered why his favorite scenery, Lutie, was not participating.

Kelvin had never seen Lutie sit anything out. Today she wasn't singing. She wasn't laughing. Her hands and eyes were not dancing. Maybe she didn't feel good. When Kelvin felt crummy, he stayed home and enjoyed a little daytime TV and a lot of ice cream.

Kelvin spotted somebody sitting in Mr. Gregg's office. Perhaps it was a superintendent, grading Mr. Gregg's teaching technique. Kelvin hoped Mr. Gregg would go easy on the soprano jokes in front of a stranger. The music teacher loved to insult the sopranos, who usually had the melody, the easiest part, and failed pitifully if they were challenged.

Energy poured off Mr. Gregg like rain in a storm of excitement. Kids loved to be around him, as if they'd been thirsty all day and he was their drink of cold water. He even had extra tenors clamoring to get into concert choir. In most schools, tenors would rather be dead than admit that they were tenors, never mind go sing in an actual choir.

"Got a new piece!" Mr. Gregg shouted. He always raised his voice, as if his best musicians had hearing problems. "Sopranos, you actually have to *work* on this one."

Without looking at her, Mr. Gregg handed the music to the pianist.

Kelvin looked, because the pianist was as lovely as Lutie. Doria Bell was elegant, always dressed in black, something lean and mature, as if she had just stepped out of a corporate attorney's office.

Kelvin glanced at the new sheet music. The piano part had a scary-looking introduction. But Doria would sight-read it without making a mistake. She would play the piano expressively, but her face would have no expression. Kelvin wondered now and then if there was a person inside Doria or if she was just a recording.

Doria Bell sat bolt upright on the piano bench. Her posture was always vertical. It was one of her flaws: she could not unbend.

Doria had figured it was a little flaw, hardly worth thinking about. But moving to Court Hill had been the shock of her life. She had always had friends. She had never even thought about having to make friends; they were always there. Well, she'd been here three months, and every single text message she'd gotten had been from someone a thousand miles away.

She had counted on chorus to be the source of new friends. But no. The accompanist was furniture; she came with the piano.

Oh, people were nice. Courtesy ruled in the South. But she could not step into their lives. Here she was, bursting with conversations she wanted to have and laughter she wanted to share. But there was nobody to talk to or laugh with.

School had been in session for ten weeks. Doria had never

moved before. Clearly her plan to have best friends in ten days—in fact, she had expected to have best friends in ten hours—was silly. Perhaps even ten weeks was silly. Maybe it took ten months. *There* was a hideous thought.

Her eyes fell on Lutie Painter.

Lutie was a star soloist, here and in her church. Since moving to the South, Doria had begun listening to gospel. Women who sang gospel had muscular voices that shouted down the aisle. Lutie did not need to shout. From her small frame came a voice stronger than that of a grown woman with a lot more inches, pounds and years: rich melted chocolate with no weak spots and no breaking points. Lutie could blend with the wispiest voice or produce enough volume to be heard over all eighty singers in the choir.

Doria thought Lutie probably had perfect pitch, as she herself did. It would be a statistical rarity for two kids out of eighty to have perfect pitch. But Lutie also had perfect pitch for friendship, Doria thought. How did she do it? Absolutely everybody liked her.

Reluctantly, Doria glanced at the music Mr. Gregg had not bothered to give her ahead of time. Mr. Gregg did not perform entry-level, easy-note stuff. He liked to brag about Doria, telling other music teachers how lucky he was to have this outstanding accompanist.

Doria would think, Fine, but I'm alone on the piano bench while everybody else is sitting in a row making friends.

She opened the music. A non-pianist would think the piano part was complex, but all those sixteenth notes were just chord outlines. The left hand had a fun jazzy beat, and the eight-measure intro had a few tricky accidentals, but she read them as easily as she read English.

Doria hated practicing the piano, which was not her instrument. Her theory was: get it right the first time, which saves you the trouble of practicing. She was always puzzled by slow learners in the chorus. Why didn't they just get it right the first time too?

I bet that's another flaw, she thought. People know that I think they should learn faster and easier. I wonder how many flaws I have that back home they didn't notice or were used to?

Mr. Gregg lifted his arms for the downbeat. Doria forgot everything else and entered the music: brain, eyes, fingers, arms and soul. She did not surface until the last note.

"Good sight-reading," said Mr. Gregg, meaning the chorus. He rarely made eye contact with Doria; you didn't have to pay attention to perfection. "Baritones," he yelled, "from the top."

Doria gave the baritones their starting note. It was now reasonable for her to look at the boys, so she raised her eyes and studied the second row. Don't look too long, she reminded herself.

She could not make an ordinary friend, but she was drowning in an unexpected crush. The crush was so physical. Her throat thickened when she saw him. Her lungs gave out, her heart raced, her eyes glazed, her speech stumbled.

At least she could still play the piano. She banged out the baritone part. Nobody looked her way. A pianist was wallpaper.

When she had first moved here, she might as well have been deaf wallpaper, too. She could hardly understand a word. Half the student body had also moved to Court Hill from somewhere else, and their English was just English. But the local white kids drawled, making each word mysterious and thick. The local black kids used a sort of shorthand, omitting syllables and skipping important parts of sentences.

Sometimes she wanted to scream at her parents, "How

could you do this to me? I had friends at home. Now you've thrown me to these slow-speaking wolves. How am I ever going to have friends in this place? I can't even tell what they're talking about."

Doria had given up trying to understand her classmates, and just let their speech pour over her. Their Southern lilt was like chamber music: like tiny concerts all over the place. Except for the swearing, of course. In that way, Court Hill High was exactly like her New England high school: the same four-letter words shouted down the halls. Dead words that did not vibrate or sing.

And then one day, Doria found that she understood every word. It was like being a spy. They thought they were talking Romanian and could say anything around strangers and it would still be a secret—but Doria, a Yankee stranger, was now in on it.

And so what?

Who cared about anything if you didn't have friends?

Teaching the baritones their part was a one-finger activity. With her free hand, Doria slid her cell phone out of her purse and texted Nell back home. Just moving her thumb, just pressing Send, knowing that Nell loved hearing from her and would answer, was strengthening.

Gazing on my crush, Doria wrote. *K is perfect.*

Mr. Gregg did not think Kelvin was perfect. "Kelvin!" he yelled.

"Yes, sir!" Kelvin was grinning. Mr. Gregg loved to tease him because Kelvin could take it, whereas other kids might be destroyed by teasing. Kelvin never understood that. But then, he had always laughed more easily than most.

"Kelvin, in this chorus, we sit up in our chairs. We do not

28

lean back. We do not cross our legs. We do not daydream. What are you, anyway—a soprano?"

"Okay. Want me to switch? I can sing falsetto."

"You can have my seat, Kelvin," called one of the girls. "I'd love to sit with the baritones."

Everyone laughed except Lutie. Lutie, who usually radiated happiness the way some kids radiated despair. Kelvin would corner her later on to see what was wrong.

One good thing, though: poor old Doria was laughing with the rest.

Whatever Doria consisted of—certainly Kelvin didn't know; he had briefly been in a chemistry class with her until their teacher had said, "Wow," and moved Doria into the honors section—she'd be better off adding laughter to her repertoire instead of Beethoven.

Kelvin gave Doria a special grin and the poor thing blushed and dropped her eyes.

$\backsim$

Doria had been in Kelvin's chemistry class for a short time. The teacher had scolded Kelvin continually: "Kelvin, stop talking." "Kelvin, keep your thoughts to yourself." "Kelvin, turn off your phone." "Kelvin, I would like somebody else's opinion for a change." Kelvin would roar with laughter. His laugh lifted the whole class and broke into little laughing pieces around the room. Doria sometimes felt as if she could pick up the pieces and carry them home.

Kelvin did not even sit quietly. He and Lutie—both Class-A people persons—would do waist-up dances while sitting in class, or hand and arm dances, and sometimes just chin dances. Whereas Doria, dancing, could hardly be seen moving.

If asked, Doria would have said that when she fell in love,

29

it would be with a boy similar to herself: quiet, contained and studious.

She would have said it would be with a boy who loved her back.

But Kelvin liked everybody. Over a thousand kids in this building, and he turned the same warmth and the same smile on everyone.

But above all, she would have expected him to be white.

That he wasn't was a surprise she yearned to talk about. She would look at the girls in choir whose names she knew but who were not her girlfriends, and imagine having girlfriend conversations with them about Kelvin. There could be no more compelling topic. She would not immediately state her interest, which was reaching the level of obsession, but would calmly and casually ask if they'd always been in school with him.

In her desperation to make friends, last Sunday Doria had gone to Youth Group at the church her parents attended, the same church where she practiced the organ after school. First Methodist. Back home, Youth Group was for losers. Maybe a category even lower than loser.

Since having zero friends meant that Doria was already a loser, and since she had a job that marked her out as a loser, she was not eager to be in this category yet again.

Doria was an organist with her own church job in the city. Church organists might as well wear jackets embroidered "Dork." Being an organist was not a ticket to friends, like, say, being a flutist. If you played the flute, you could join marching band, which was cool, though not very. But playing the organ was just another way of sitting alone. Nor did a pipe organ give you any sexy lines to utter. "Want to hear some Bach?" did not bring people running.

Doria gathered her courage and launched herself at the Methodist Youth Group, expecting that it too was Dork City, but willing to give it a try. The Youth Group space had foosball, table tennis and a half gym for volleyball or dances. It had great furniture for slouching on, and they had ordered every possible type of pizza, with toppings Doria would never have tested on her own, like pineapple and chicken.

To her relief, Rebecca, who was in concert choir and honors chemistry with her, was in Youth Group, and so was Jenny, another soprano.

But instead of playing games during which Doria might find a partner and make inroads to friendship, the kids were forced to listen to some woman named Miss Kendra talk about her hot meal ministry. Of course, in the South people were so polite you couldn't tell what they really thought. They sat with their cheerful expressions and their nice posture and Doria tried to imitate them.

It seemed that every Saturday morning, Miss Kendra prepared—in her own kitchen, on an ordinary stove—enough food for a hundred people. Then she drove into poor neighborhoods and served dinner right out of her car to anybody who walked up hungry.

Doria was impressed. No soup kitchen in town? Fine. I'll do it myself. Doria wanted to be just like that—stopped by nothing.

Miss Kendra had come to Youth Group because she needed volunteers. Everybody's hand went up. It sounded so fun.

Except—where were these poor neighborhoods? Court Hill looked pretty prosperous to Doria. It was a difficult town to get a hold on. Everything was brand-new and weirdly identical. It was strewn with housing developments, each with a cute name emblazoned on a brick wall. Half the streets weren't even on GPS yet. There was nothing local about Court Hill: its features were more like national currency—they could be spent anywhere and nobody would notice a difference. CVS and Walmart and Target and Rite-Aid and all the other pharmacy chains and box stores and groceries were so regularly spaced that you didn't measure in miles; you measured by stores.

Doria couldn't think of anyplace she would consider poor, where there were actual hungry people.

Miss Kendra beamed at all those hands in the air. But she wanted only one volunteer at a time. "We don't go into a neighborhood like an army," she explained. "When we serve meals, there's me and my husband, Mr. Billy, because I don't drive into Chalk unless there's a man along, and then I like two other people. One has to be an adult, but one of you kids would be a great help next Saturday."

Doria wanted to laugh when Miss Kendra referred to her husband as "Mr. Billy," which sounded like the name of a goat in a nursery rhyme, but it was the local style. Children here grew up calling their friends' dads Mr. Nick or Mr. Jason. They called their Sunday-school teachers Miss Joanne or Miss Katy. Doria couldn't go there. It was like the way they called their male teachers "sir" and their female teachers "ma'am." It didn't sound polite to Doria. It sounded like a military academy.

She wondered what Chalk was. Presumably not the stuff with which little kids wrote on sidewalks.

When the Youth Group realized that only one of them was wanted for this volunteer opportunity, they lost interest. Only Doria's hand was still up, making her the sole volunteer for next Saturday.

There was no way out.

She couldn't say to Miss Kendra, I don't actually care about you and your mission. I don't want to do good. I just want a friend.

Now, in chorus, Doria entered the music, which was so much easier than entering a social life. The baritones were history. Now she played the alto part, the tenor part, the soprano part, and finally all four together. This stumped most pianists. It was hard to read four staves. Doria did it all the time and hardly noticed.

⌒

Lutie was so sorry she had come back to school after her shocking morning. The shadowy figure of the professor inside the music office was a threat. It tangled her mind, as if she didn't have enough knots and shreds thinking about Saravette.

Of course when she was desperate for chorus to end, Mr. Gregg dismissed them late. The next class, Music Appreciation, was coming into the big music room before the chorus had even stopped singing.

In previous years, bored kids who needed an easy credit signed up for Music Appreciation. This year, another type had enrolled. Train's type.

Train Greene was trouble. He lived on a street where drugs ruled, and he planned to be one of the rulers, like his brother before him. His big brother, DeRade, had finally gotten the prison sentence he'd been working on for so long, and now it was Train who was preparing for prison, the way Lutie was preparing for college.

The older Greene brother had been a pit bull, a boy who should have been on a chain but instead roamed the neighborhood, biting children. DeRade developed a taste for twisting arms, and broke one or two. He not only kicked dogs, he ran after them in order to kick them. It was something when a junkyard dog was afraid of a kid.

Train had not caught up to the level DeRade had achieved at his age, but Lutie figured it was only a matter of days. Train was seventeen now and six foot two. He'd been pretty hefty for a while, well over two hundred pounds, and a football-team wannabe. Train had not made the team. Perhaps that was what had made him so angry.

Train had lost weight in the months since DeRade went to jail. He now had the thin tight look of a starving animal. His eyes blazed feverishly. Lutie figured dogs with rabies had eyes like that.

Train buzzed into the music room like a hornet. People looked elsewhere, because making eye contact with Train wasn't good. They stepped aside quickly, because blocking Train wasn't good.

If Train had made the football team, thought Lutie, he'd be at practice every afternoon. If they weren't going to confine him to jail, they could at least confine him to the gym.

The professor emerged from Mr. Gregg's office. What a contrast the two men were: blustery red-cheeked yellow-haired Mr. Gregg, his shirt untucked and his tie askew; slim trim ebony Professor Durham, looking like a guest on a Wall Street talk show. They seemed unaware of the chaos caused by the boy formerly known as Cliff Greene.

Doria got up from the piano bench. Train stuck out a huge foot, his white sneaker filthy and his laces dangling. Doria stumbled on it, Train withdrew it quickly, smiling, and Doria lurched into the line of exiting sopranos. Her books and music—the ugly yellow plastic briefcase she always carried, and her little red purse, which she had forgotten to zip—flew out of her hands. From the purse shot coins, pencils, a cell phone, Chap Stick and keys that hung from a brass treble clef chain.

Only Lutie, stranded in the top row while the sopranos dawdled, saw that Train had tripped Doria on purpose. Rebecca and Jenny, closer to the door, just saw clumsy Doria. Sighing, they paused to retrieve Doria's scattered belongings. Train stooped and picked up Doria's key chain. He held it by the brass treble clef, swinging the keys too high for Doria to reach. Train loved to withhold things. "Lots of keys," he said, in the creepy taunting voice he had begun using this year.

Train and DeRade had a nice mother, and although DeRade had never been nice, Train had been sweet when he was little. Miss Veola—whose church Train had attended until he'd gotten too big for his mama to order him around—believed that if she could just separate Train from bad influences, he would return to being nice.

Lutie did not believe that.

Kids like Train were not making choices about being nice; they were making choices about getting attention. Nice kids were noticed by their mothers. Vicious kids were noticed by everybody. DeRade Greene was famous. Train wanted the same. He too wanted some girl to say admiringly, "You the baddest."

Train jangled the keys in the air. "You the super for an apartment building, Doria?"

Doria shook her head. "Thank you for picking up my keys," she said, all Yankee and prim, holding out her hand.

Train kept the keys out of reach, separating two of them. "Car keys," he identified. "The other seven?"

Lutie elbowed her way forward down the risers.

Once they had all been friends—Kelvin and Lutie and Cliff, before anybody had thought of calling him Train. They got off the school bus at the same stop near Chalk. Lutie would walk all the way to Peter Creek and hop from rock to rock across the water. Sometimes she fell in. Then she'd slime home to MeeMaw, who would say, "Girl, either improve your balance or get off at the next stop instead and use the bridge!"

Last year, after a homicide, Train's brother was picked up by the police. Somebody had ratted on DeRade. People in Chalk did not talk to the police; it was a lapse of judgment on the part of a kid who thought he was helping society. The police didn't have enough evidence to keep DeRade. He was out in a day and went straight for the kid who'd ratted on him. Poor Nate got himself packed in barbed wire one night and lost an eye.

The barbed wire had been cut right out of the fence in DeRade and Train's backyard. Nobody had mended it. The big rectangle was still there, sagging on both sides. Since DeRade boasted about getting Nate, it was easier to put him in jail this time, and eventually he got the years in prison he'd been hoping for.

Everybody knew that Train had been along. But DeRade didn't give his brother up, and Nate, who had learned a hard lesson, told the police it had been very dark out and he hadn't seen his attacker.

He really couldn't see now.

Lutie thought of Saravette, who hung twenty-four hours a day with people like DeRade. Who might *be* a person like DeRade.

"House keys," said Doria, so brainless that she pointed them out to Train. "And church keys."

Train looked repelled. "Church keys?" Then he laughed. "Which church?"

Lutie didn't like this. Churches had terrific music equipment—high-quality electric keyboards and guitars, drums and microphones. Recording gear. In church offices were computers and printers, and in old Sunday-school rooms, air-conditioning units.

If you planned to steal, you wanted a building to be empty. But if you were looking for entertainment, which was more up Train's alley, you might want to enter when somebody was there. Somebody like Doria.

Alone.

Jenny handed over Doria's fallen cell phone and said in her high, carrying soprano, "Doria, is it true that you practice the organ in that big old church every day by yourself? You're alone in the dark with the music?"

Telling Train that here was a girl who stayed alone and unsafe in the dark of an empty building? And by the way, you're holding the key?

Finally Lutie arrived on the scene. She plucked the key ring from Train's hand, tucked it into Doria's purse, zipped the purse closed, hooked her arm in Doria's and said over her shoulder, "She's never alone, Jenny. What idiot would be alone in a big empty building? Come on, Doria, we're late for lunch."

Kelvin believed that Train needed to be on strong medication.

Of all the boys who had dropped out of school—this was a school system where less than two-thirds of kindergartners would be onstage to receive a high school diploma twelve years later—what a puzzle that Train still attended. Even more amazing that he remained at large in a neighborhood like Chalk, where a quarter of the young men either had been or were now in juvenile detention or jail, and his own brother was serving a prison sentence. You would have expected him to drop out in eighth grade, go straight to drug-dealing and die young.

When Kelvin and Train—Cliff, back then—were little,

they had gone to the same church. Kelvin had memories of them both getting Sunday-school attendance pins.

Every Sunday, Miss Veola prayed for her young men: Lord, keep them in school. Keep them righteous. Keep them safe. Keep them from doing bad things. And if they do bad things, keep them from harming others.

She was a realist, Miss Veola. She didn't pretend there was no evil in the world. She didn't pretend there was no evil in Chalk.

African American ministers made a great effort to get their teenage boys off the road to prison and onto the road of ordinary lives, but the trouble was—who wanted to be ordinary? Jobs, mortgages, lawn mowing? What was the attraction?

Even Kelvin didn't want those.

Kelvin's parents felt that most evil came from drugs. Every day of Kelvin's life, his parents would demand to know who his friends were. "Pretty much everybody," Kelvin would say.

"And Quander? You friends with Quander?" his mom asked.

"Yes, ma'am," he would tell his mother. "I like Quander. I know he's into stuff, but I'm not doing it with him. I promise."

Kelvin's father was an administrator at the hospital, where he ran the public clinics for things like AIDS and detox. He knew the world at its saddest and roughest. "I love that you love everybody, Kelvin," his daddy would say. "But be careful. It's easy to fall into step with people you shouldn't even be near."

Kelvin felt insulated by his own personality. The easygoing types of this world didn't have to be careful.

When Lutie linked her arm with Doria's, Kelvin's heart turned over. Lutie was the nicest person in the world. It was no small thing to take Doria Bell to lunch. Doria was like the subject of a nasty jump rope rhyme: *Loser, loser—how you gonna use her?*

But Lutie did not plan to use Doria. She was just being kind.

Kelvin fell madly in love with her.

Of course, he did this daily.

Kelvin too slouched off to lunch.

Doria was elated. Lutie was taking her to lunch! Just as surprising, Rebecca fell in step and walked on Doria's other side, making them a trio.

Lutie set a fast pace, which was unusual. Popular girls sauntered so friends could catch up. Popular girls traveled in groups.

Rebecca spoke first. "Listen to me, Doria. Stay away from Train. As for church, if you *do* practice alone in the dark—stop."

Doria despised being given advice, but she nodded as if she were grateful. As it happened, there were few things she liked more than being alone in the dark with the music.

A pipe organ could make a serious racket. When Doria practiced, a Scout troop could set up camp in the church and she wouldn't hear. She had to learn prelude, offertory and postlude every week, plus hymns, choir anthem and responses. She concentrated better in an empty church. When there were people around, she became a performer, showing off instead of practicing.

She hadn't meant to be a church organist. She'd never come across anybody who had. You got drafted when your church found out you played the piano well and they could turn you into a Sunday substitute on that somewhat similar instrument, the organ.

There were two bonuses to being a church organist. You had an audience every week; Doria loved an audience. And they paid you; Doria loved earning an income.

Rebecca, Lutie and Doria reached the cafeteria. Three sets

of double doors were propped open. Kids from all four grades were entering and leaving, talking and laughing, yelling and shoving. The three girls were separated by the motion of the crowds.

Although every class and activity at Court Hill High had black, white, Hispanic and a sprinkling of Asian students, at lunch the races tended not to mix. Doria struggled to get through the cafeteria door, while Lutie joined a crush of noisy laughing black girls and Rebecca glided across the room to share a chair at a table of white girls.

Lunch was now exactly what it was every other school day: Doria standing alone without a place to sit.

She could have pretended Lutie had meant it when she said, "Come on, we're late for lunch," and walked over to that table. Doria would be the only white girl there. Southerners were courteous, and Doria doubted that anybody would be rude, but they would be surprised, and the fact was, Lutie was looking in the opposite direction and did not seem to be extending an invitation.

Doria was not insightful, but it occurred to her suddenly and painfully that Lutie had not been seeking her company: she had been separating Doria from Train. Nor had Rebecca been launching a friendship: Rebecca was just giving orders.

⟡

Around Lutie, girls talked loudly and laughed even more loudly. Sometimes Lutie thought the whole point of lunch was not to eat food, but to let kids make noise.

In the far right corner lounged boys who were bigger, burlier and more tattooed than most. In fact, they were men who happened to attend high school: Train and his rivals. Sometimes allies, sometimes at each other's throats. Literally.

The teachers on cafeteria duty had arranged themselves on the opposite side of the large room, hoping distance would save them from having to deal with that bunch.

On her cell phone, Lutie went to the Internet and looked up the Ten Commandments, even though she knew them by heart. She read them slowly. She could not imagine Saravette caring about most of them. Saravette had probably taken the Lord's name in vain, for example, a million times.

But maybe even Saravette was bothered by breaking the Do Not Kill rule.

Saravette had turned her infant girl over to her own mother straight from the hospital and never once pretended that she was anybody's mother. Instead, Lutie had had four mothers in her sixteen years: MeeMaw, Aunt Grace, Aunt Tamika and Miss Veola.

But Saravette was a mother.

Lutie's.

Lord, don't let my mother be a killer, she thought. Tell me Saravette just broke nine of those commandments.

⁃

Doria was still frozen in the doorway when Rebecca waved.

Doria was embarrassed by how grateful she was. In a moment, she was next to Rebecca and across from Jenny. How safe a person felt, sitting between other people. Alone on a piano or organ bench, Doria had a job and a purpose. But alone anywhere else, Doria felt like a stick, a piece of kindling about to be thrown into the fire. She could go up in smoke and nobody would notice.

"You're not eating, Doria?" said Rebecca. "You didn't buy any lunch? Here. Have some of my apple slices."

Doria had written Rebecca off after getting marching

orders about practicing alone. But here she was being kind and thoughtful. "Thank you," said Doria humbly. She nibbled an apple slice. It was crisp and sugary and made her want to cry.

Jenny leaned across the table. "Last Sunday evening? When Miss Kendra spoke? You were so brave to volunteer, Doria."

"Brave?"

"Well . . . Chalk," said Jenny, making a face. "I mean, the police are down there every five minutes. There's a shoot-out every weekend."

I'm going someplace where there's a shoot-out every weekend? thought Doria.

Jenny sniffed. "We wouldn't even have a homicide rate in Court Hill if it weren't for Chalk." She looked irritated. Like, homicide rates are *so* annoying.

"Chalk?" repeated another girl, sounding astonished. "You couldn't pay me."

She's telling the truth, thought Doria. If I gave her money, she wouldn't go to this place called Chalk. So back at Youth Group, the other kids didn't lower their hands because only one person could volunteer. They backed out because they would never go to Chalk either.

What was Chalk? And where?

All these months, Doria had failed to encounter the Old South. There were differences between New England and here, but fewer than Doria had expected. Her new town had the same houses, with the same cars in the same driveways and the same people with the same lives, joys and worries. Some of the flowers and trees were different, and it was hotter in summer, and yes, restaurant service and traffic were slower—but nothing seemed to be "old." In fact, everything here was brand-new. It was the North that was burdened by old stuff.

Across the room, Doria saw Kelvin. Her crush seemed to

come out of the floor and envelop her. She had a sudden fear that she would leap up from the table and cry, "Kelvin! Over here! It's me!"

Kelvin was using his cell phone. She could see his thumb move. She was just pretending the text was for her when she really did receive a message. Her heart leaped with hope. Kelvin! Maybe he too had fallen in love across the music room!

She fumbled like a person who had never used a phone.

Rebecca laughed. "For the first time, I can tell you're a soprano, Doria."

But the message was from Mr. Gregg. Doria flushed. She had actually let herself believe that Kelvin would text her. The girls leaned forward to see, texts being public property.

Come see me ASAP.

Who cared what a music teacher in his forties wanted? And what was up with "As Soon As Possible"? There is no such thing as a music emergency. Doria was not walking away from her first chance at making friends, even though one of them seemed to think murder was simply an annoyance.

"I bet it's about the musical," said Jenny. "I know you're working on it with him."

Mr. Gregg had been trying for years now to write his own high school musical. He insisted that this spring it would actually be performed. Doria doubted it. He had played his songs for her more than once. The music was derivative and dull and she thought that in his heart, Mr. Gregg knew. How painful that must be. To dream and dream and dream, knowing deep down that you didn't have what it took. Doria felt weirdly protective of Mr. Gregg. It would not be from her that he learned the truth.

"Is it true he's writing the lead for Lutie?" asked Jenny. "Or is there a chance for other people?" Jenny looked around, obviously hoping somebody would nominate her as the best possible lead.

But Rebecca said, "You should try out, Doria. There'll be a pit band for the performance, so you won't have to play the piano. You have a beautiful voice, more soprano-y than Lutie's. Lutie is an alto who happens to sing high."

Doria could not imagine a worse description of Lutie's extraordinary voice. "Nobody could compete with Lutie," she said matter-of-factly.

"Go see Mr. Gregg right now," urged Jenny.

"I haven't even bought my lunch yet."

"Go. There's time. Then come back and tell us," said Rebecca. "I bet two Girl Scout cookies that you are going to do something special on that musical."

Doria laughed. "What kind of Girl Scout cookies? I would only make an effort for Thin Mints."

Rebecca held up Thin Mints.

The music room could be approached by a quiet back hall lined with stage entrances, a prop room, a scenery room, bathrooms and, of course, the storage room. Doria loved that room—crowded and messy and full of music books and CD collections and sheet music and the school-owned tuba in need of repair and the old electric keyboards, not worth using but worth too much to toss.

Doria received another text. It was from Nell.

She and Nell had met when they were six, their piano lessons scheduled back to back. Nell dropped piano in middle school when she began violin, and dropped violin when she began high school, because orchestra just didn't compete with all the other great stuff she could do in high school. The orchestra teacher almost wept. There are never enough violin players, and Nell was good. Nell shrugged. "I don't have time for everything," she said dismissively.

But she always had time for Doria.

Nell would change her class schedule to be in Doria's section. Coax the whole basketball team to attend Doria's recitals. Drag Doria shopping, and force her to buy clothing in colors other than black. Phone her on a school-day morning and demand a view via cell phone so she could judge what Doria had draped on her body and whether it was acceptable.

Doria pressed View to read the text message.

She was sure that by now Nell would have gone to the Facebook page for Court Hill High's concert choir and identified the only "K" in chorus. Now that Doria had shared the big event in her life—well, actually, the big nonevent—she and Nell could have some real girl talk about a really great guy.

But Nell's text, mostly abbreviations and smiles, was an update on her own situation, involving teachers and kids Doria had never met. The message could have been meant for anyone.

Doria brought up Nell's last few messages. They were all like that. She's texting me out of habit, thought Doria. I could move back there and we'd be friends again, but I'm far away, in another place, and I'm getting smaller and smaller in Nell's life.

Doria's feet had carried her to the music room.

Music Appreciation was still going, and the kids were still unappreciative. The class was being taught by a small tidy African American man far more formally dressed than the usual male teacher. Mr. Gregg zoomed over to Doria, coming so close that she had to back up, until they were in the quiet hall, invisible to the class and the unknown teacher.

Jenny and Rebecca had been wrong—Mr. Gregg was not

45

thinking about his own music. He was concerned with lost folk music—a group of songs bizarrely known to music historians as the Laundry List. Nobody knew what these were, or even if they existed. Some academic types believed that the Laundry List had originated with the Painter family, right here in Court Hill.

And you're telling me because . . . ? thought Doria.

"Lutie is a Painter," said Mr. Gregg excitedly. "She claims not to know anything about the Laundry List. But she knows."

The intensity with which he said this was unsettling.

"I didn't realize you were friends with Lutie until she grabbed your arm and took you to lunch," said Mr. Gregg. "That's great, Doria. Sometimes I despair that we're ever really going to integrate. Cafeteria tables and church pews are the last bastions of segregation. The trouble is, in both those situations, everybody wants to segregate. I just love it that you've crossed that barrier. Now listen. Get those songs out of Lutie. Tell her you'll play the piano for her or something."

Doria loved her music teacher. She loved studying composition with him. She loved when Mr. Gregg said, "Doria, someday I'll be able to say I knew you when." But she did not love this creepy eagerness, this back-room order to snatch something from Lutie that Lutie must not want to hand over. Or didn't have to start with.

"I need those songs, Doria," said Mr. Gregg, his voice gravelly with want. "They're my ticket out."

4

The last class of her school day was chemistry. Doria could read chemistry as easily as music. When the teacher asked a question that afternoon, Doria replied without needing to think.

Since this teacher never called on anybody twice, Doria stopped paying attention and just soaked up the music of the teacher's voice. The woman was from coastal Carolina, which she called the Low Country, as if it were one, like Holland. Her speech had a lovely lilt, some words slurred and others hummed.

Outside, rain crashed on the roofs of cars, slammed on the pavement and flooded low-lying areas. It created mud, serious mud, as if all that red Carolina dirt had been hoping to surface and today was the day.

Doria held her cell phone in her hand, and her hand rested in her lap, protected by the desk. She wanted to tell Nell a thousand things, but a text message was mostly good for one or two things.

These days, Doria mainly connected with Nell and with Stephanie, her other best friend, on Facebook or by text message. It was not satisfying. If she wrote about chorus (*Mr. Gregg is excellent*) and the other sopranos (*This girl Lutie has an amazing voice*) and her organ teacher (*very civilized compared to my last one, all that screaming and spitting*), Stephanie and Nell would write back, *You don't have to pretend people down there have anything to offer* or *Come on, if the teacher's that good, he'd be in a decent school.*

She ached for the company of Nell and Stephanie, but at the same time, the thought of communicating with them exhausted her.

Instead, staring out at the weather, she composed a rain symphony in her mind, melody and chords with the slithery dissonance of slick mud. When she got home tonight, she'd use a computer program to write it down, although sometimes she liked a pencil and staff paper.

What had Mr. Gregg meant by "my ticket out"?

He was doing a stellar job at a big thriving high school, and was often asked to bring his impressive concert choir to nationwide choral conferences as a demonstration group. He had outstanding parental support, and even in pinched times, the school board gave his music program whatever money it needed.

Maybe it was the town of Court Hill he wanted out of.

Doria could see that. This wasn't New York. In fact, it was nowhere. But the Lord had created a lot of fine musicians, and in Court Hill Doria felt elbow to elbow with many of them.

When her family had announced their plan to move down here, people had said, "Oh, please—the *South*? It's such a retarded part of the world. Who will you even talk to? As for music, the poor things probably don't have any. You going to strum a banjo?" And when Doria insisted that music was top-notch at Court Hill High, they replied, "You don't have to pretend. We know it's second-rate on a good day."

48

Did Mr. Gregg agree?

But how could songs from Lutie's family be anybody's ticket anywhere, let alone Mr. Gregg's?

Across from Doria, in the same science classroom, Lutie raised her hand, was called on and answered correctly. Now she too could think her own thoughts.

She had received a text message from her pastor. She didn't want to open it.

With all the expansion in Court Hill, there was also collapse. The old single-screen movie theater had undergone extensive remodeling in an attempt to attract viewers. It had struggled for years, and when it had closed for good, Veola Mixton had bought it. (Well, technically the church had voted to buy it, but only because Miss Veola insisted.)

The theater held several hundred people in comfy seats, and had excellent heating and air-conditioning. The lobby was perfect for coffee hour. There was a tiny office and good restrooms. Miss Veola planned to remove the front rows, put in an altar and a pulpit, hang a cross where the screen had been and she'd be good to go.

"You don't have a big enough congregation," people said scornfully.

"The Lord will fill it," said Miss Veola, who always spoke as if the Lord obeyed her and not the other way around. To Lutie, she had said, "You'll be my star attraction. I'm going to have you sing the Laundry List for the first fund-raiser. With the Lord's help, our church will serve both black and white neighbors."

"Black and white neighbors don't want the same church," said Lutie.

"Nonsense. We have to mix populations. All Christians—

49

African American, white, Hispanic, Asian—we've isolated ourselves. I want us in the same room on Sunday morning. Right now there's only one thing every church in Court Hill agrees on and that's Jesus' name."

It was true. There was a church on every corner and they were all suspicious of each other.

"We figure anybody who believes less than we do is pitiful and weak, and anybody who believes more is deranged," Miss Veola said. "Now, Lutie, let's start planning the publicity for your concert."

"I'm not giving a concert. Why don't you design a great T-shirt? Who doesn't want another T-shirt?"

"Lutie! Even a church in a movie theater isn't going to get much publicity. But the Laundry List? Honey, every radio station, newspaper, local TV show and historical society will be on board. Symphony people and arty people and bluegrass people—they'll all be excited! The stories I'll tell about Mabel Painter, and about your MeeMaw, and the previews we'll do of your singing—what an audience we'll have! I just need those people once, Lutie. They see how we make the Word of God come to life, and they'll be back."

All that publicity—and Lutie would star.

All those people buying tickets—to hear her.

All that recording equipment—to preserve Lutie Painter's voice.

It was tempting. But Lutie said no. "MeeMaw told me a hundred times that some people inherit land, but we inherited songs. She said, *You hold Mabel Painter's songs tight, baby girl. You put them in your heart and you keep them there.*"

"And you have, Lutie. But now it's time to share them. That kind of beauty belongs to everyone, like some kind of national park."

The songs did not belong to everybody. They belonged to Lutie.

Lutie's grandmother, and great-grandmother, and great-great-grandmother had had to look up for hope, because they sure hadn't found much on the ground in Chalk. When those women had looked at the sky, they'd seen stairs to heaven. When Lutie looked up, she saw weather patterns and knowledge gained from space exploration. Miss Veola said heaven was a different sphere, a plane of existence known only to those who lived in the Lord.

When Lutie sang the songs, either she believed as deeply as her MeeMaw or she didn't believe at all. Either way, it made her cry. Mabel Painter's shouts to God were not spirituals in which the singer rocked in the arms of Jesus. Mabel was stuck on earth, starching and ironing in the summer heat.

> *Big sky*
> *Hard sky*
> *Sky of small cold stars*
> *You got a star for me, Lord?*
> *So far all I got is scars.*
> *I need a star, Lord.*
> *Come shine for me, Lord.*
> *Why you so far, Lord?*

Inside that song were the thousand hurts and cuts of a life of drudgery. And for what? For children and grandchildren whose lives did not improve, in spite of Mabel's sacrifices.

To Lutie, the song of cold stars was like a psalm. Psalm 13, say. Psalm 22. Time out of mind, people had cried out in sorrow and sweat, begging God to come.

Lutie did not want to sing the songs for strangers. She did not want to present her exhausted pleading great-great-grandmother for their entertainment.

Now, in chemistry, Lutie's thumb hovered over her cell phone.

Miss Veola's messages were always terse, as if every letter she entered was one less dollar to feed the poor. Today's message had one word.

Stop.

It meant "Stop in at my house and visit me."

If Professor Martin Durham was a good researcher, then he had already arrived in Chalk, because somebody would have told him that the person likeliest to know the Laundry List was Miss Veola, dearest friend of Eunice Painter, descendant of Mabel, Lutie's MeeMaw, and singer of songs from her porch.

How Miss Veola would love Professor Durham. She would see him as a gift from God for her new church. She was probably serving the man iced tea right now. She would expect Lutie to stop by and sing every verse of—

Lutie came to her senses. Miss Veola's message had nothing to do with Professor Durham. This was about skipping school. The office had finally gotten around to dealing with the absentee list. Lutie had not entered by the front door, so nobody knew she'd been in school since eleven. They had probably called Miss Veola.

The pastor would go on a real tear if she found out Lutie had gone by herself to meet her drug-addled mother.

Miss Veola had tried so hard to save Saravette. She was still trying.

She'll always try, thought Lutie. But it's too late. Saravette has broken all the commandments.

Kelvin's last class was also chemistry, but he was not in the honors section. He liked science, but not enough to get involved. He was, he decided, a C-plus person all around. Just a fraction above average, and happy to be there.

When the bell rang, Kelvin didn't race out of the room like everybody else. Kelvin was never in a hurry. He moseyed along, enjoying the scenery, which was all he ever did.

But suddenly Train blocked the corridor.

Not good. Everybody knew that Train was under orders from DeRade to go off the track. Kelvin did not want to be there when it happened. He sensed desperation in Train's hot jittery presence. Train probably felt cornered. He needed to catch up to DeRade or else surpass him. What surpassed blinding somebody? Kelvin didn't want to go there.

He thought of Nate, who had only one eye. Maybe he had a glass eye. Maybe the dead one was still there but drying up. Maybe they'd sewn his eyelids together. Maybe Nate had a hole and a patch.

Ignoring Train or walking around him would be like challenging him to a duel, so Kelvin said pleasantly, "Hey."

"You know that girl Doria?"

"Sure do," said Kelvin, since there was no point in lying.

"She in that church alone every night?"

Kelvin didn't have the slightest idea what church Doria went to, never mind whether she went there alone, but he said, "Nah. That's the busiest church in town. They got Eldercare and Alcoholics Anonymous and a day care and softball teams and a women's club and Bible studies and I don't know what all. Parking lot's always full."

Kelvin half saluted a farewell and sauntered on, making a mental note to tell Doria to watch herself, but forgetting by the time he'd reached the end of the hall.

Thursday
Afternoon and Evening

Train falls for fire.

Doria stays a stranger.

Pierce stops a bus.

Lutie loses a song.

5

School ended.

Lutie never took the school bus home. Buses left within two minutes of the last bell, and she refused to sprint out of the building and throw herself into some smelly old vehicle. She liked to hang out, see what everybody planned to do next, have a Coke and then decide on a home. Which one did she want today?

Lutie considered going to Aunt Grace's for the night, because she felt like a restaurant, and Aunt Grace always felt like a restaurant, and they might try one of the new ones in the new shopping center, with the new menus and the new flavors.

But Aunt Grace was a suspicious soul. You didn't run a successful Department of Motor Vehicles if you were naïve. Lutie did not want Aunt Grace to find out that she had gone alone into the worst part of the city, let alone that she had gone to see Saravette. When her sister's name came up, Aunt Grace always turned her head, as if she couldn't even face the sound of the name, never mind the person who wore it.

Aunt Grace was less likely to deal with Saravette than Aunt Tamika.

Saravette would call Tamika's cell phone. Aunt Tamika would sigh, long and low, and fish in her purse for the bottle of aspirin she kept there. When the call was over, she would sit for a minute and gather herself. If Lutie asked what Saravette had said, Aunt Tamika would shrug. If Tamika drove into town to deal with Saravette, Uncle Dean usually went with her.

Sometimes it was police who called.

Aunt Tamika would be exceptionally polite to them, as if she were interviewing for a job. Then she would go off by herself and when she came back, her eyes would be red.

There were never explanations.

If Lutie presented a form for school where "parent or guardian" had to be filled in, Aunt Tamika would write her name and Uncle Dean's in such big square print that it filled the space and the margins, to prove there was absolutely no room for the name Saravette.

Lutie really did not know what Aunt Tamika would do if she found out about Lutie's trip uptown today. Her aunts and uncle had never said so—they never would—but their ruling fear was that Lutie would follow Saravette's steps instead of theirs. They were always worried about crime, which at any minute could sweep a person up because that was what crime did. "Crime is a wide broom," said Aunt Tamika, "and those little straws on the edge catch everything."

Aunt Tamika and Uncle Dean had excellent jobs at the headquarters of a national bank. They had a big beautiful home in a big beautiful subdivision called Willowmere, the prettiest word Lutie had ever heard. They dressed wonderfully. Lutie was always eager to see what neat stuff they had bought. Aunt Tamika had fabulous shoes and scarves, lots of handbags and terrific jewelry, all big, bright and spangly, like

Aunt Tamika herself. Uncle Dean had been a football player in high school and college, but now his broad shoulders were covered by fine suits in navy or charcoal, and he looked exactly like the men on television business reports, and talked like them, and worried about the same things.

Lutie loved Aunt Tamika and Uncle Dean, and she loved their house and her bedroom there, with every possible comfort times ten. It was a million miles and a million dollars from Chalk, where Tamika, Grace and Saravette had grown up.

Lutie dragged her thoughts from Saravette.

Outdoors, it rained like an upside-down river. The lobby was packed with kids waiting for the rain to end or their mothers to arrive in cars. Lutie lifted her closed umbrella. She was the only person who had one.

"Whoa, Loot! You brought an umbrella? You scared of water, girl?"

It was Train. Lutie did not want to deal with him. He had been so sweet, back when he and Lutie and Kelvin and Rebecca and Jenny had been in kindergarten together. He could still be sweet if he wanted something enough. You had to be careful. Charm could be as vicious as a knife.

Train nodded at the kids milling around, texting and phoning and begging for rides. "You seen Doria?"

Although she had just watched Doria walk out into the rain, Lutie peered intently back into the building. "I don't see her," she said. She did not risk a friendly smile. There was no telling what Train would do with a smile. Instead she lifted her phone. Texting came in handy. Nobody was offended if you texted while they were talking to you.

Lutie texted Aunt Grace, and then Aunt Tamika, and by then, Train had wandered off. He had been at the top of the class in first and second grade, especially in spelling. But now he had as much interest in academics as a flea.

There was never a good time to be on Train's GPS. But if Lutie warned Doria to be afraid—be very afraid—Doria might tell her parents. Her parents might call the school. The cops might stop by the high school to chat with Train.

The last person to discuss one of the Greene brothers with the cops was now blind in one eye.

Better would be to make sure Doria did not practice alone in the dark.

Outdoors, rain swiped Doria like the flat of some great wet hand. She turned her face up and let the rain drum on her skin.

School was so hard. Not classes; classes were easy. But school itself: that shocking clump of kids and conversation, society and loneliness, noise and silence. Most days when the push and shove of school was over, Doria would text Nell or Stephanie, for the relief of old times.

Stephanie had beaten her to it. Sweet Steph was texting Doria now, right on time.

Doria and Stephanie had met in elementary school band. Stephanie played French horn. But music was not Steph's love. She wanted to be an engineer. Her doodles were architectural and airy, spun with trestles and spans. In high school, Stephanie quit band to take more math classes. The band teacher was distraught. Horn players were scarce.

Stephanie, like Nell, had shrugged. She had other goals.

Doria felt better about her lonely day. Nell would have texted Steph and told her that their old friend Doria had a crush on K in chorus. Nell would have found not only the chorus's Facebook page, but she would have identified Kelvin and gone to his page too. Doria braced herself for Nell's analysis: "He boasts about doing nothing. If he's the best your school has to offer, move back here." Doria loved that old refrain—move back here!—but she would ignore it to defend Kelvin. He isn't the best at school, but he's the best to be around.

But Stephanie's message was generic. *WUWH. WUZup.* Wish you were here. What's up?

Normally Doria loved all the after-school walking she did, each trek a little interlude between places and activities. Today the short hike to First Methodist seemed insuperable. She hardly had the energy to hoist her shoes over the puddles and the mud.

On a gloomy day like this, little light penetrated the stained glass and entered the church. Doria did not usually turn on the lights that hung from the soaring ceiling, only the lamp over the music rack. She really would be alone in the dark.

Her actual church job was at St. Bartholomew's, twenty miles north. She didn't have her own car to drive there and in any case wouldn't waste time going back and forth. She practiced at her parents' church instead. The thing with pipe organs was, you certainly didn't have one at home to practice on.

The first Sunday after they'd moved to Court Hill, the Bells decided to try out the handsome brick church in the center of town. Her father bragged to the minister, "My daughter Doria is a brilliant organist."

Word went out. The very next week, she was asked to sub at a little country church called Wesley Chapel, way out on Lonny Creek Road. Right away her parents were suspicious of the Carolina countryside. A church in a field might have rattlesnake handlers and three-hour sermons given by crazed men with spittle around their mouths.

But Wesley Chapel was a charming church, tall and thin and tiny, with black shutters and plain glass, and pine trees right up against the windows, as if they wanted to come in too. Literally every person in the congregation came up to say hi (actually, they said "hey") and to tell Doria how wonderfully she had played and wouldn't she be their permanent organist?

You have a crummy little electronic organ, about as musical as a coffeepot, she didn't say out loud. I don't want to play it ever again. I don't want an organ job at all, and certainly not here, where everybody's a hundred years old.

She found an organ teacher through an online search of local college music faculty. Their first lesson went on until Doria was too tired to play, which had never happened before, and Mr. Bates said, "I know of an excellent job opening. You'll audition. We'll drive up Wednesday."

So there she was, in Mr. Bates's car the following Wednesday. Her parents had insisted that she text them constantly with updates, but Doria forgot. She loved the instrument the minute she sat down. Three manuals. A rich mellow sound with bright exciting mixtures. She played a toccata, her fingers flying over the keyboards, flinging the chords from one hand to the other. She got the job.

The following Sunday, she discovered that she was the youngest person in the choir loft by twenty-five years.

At her last lesson, Doria managed to admit to Mr. Bates that she was having a hard time making friends.

"Some people aren't good at being kids," he said. "It usually means they'll be good at being grown-ups. You are so grown up, Doria. I can certainly imagine a gulf between you and the other kids, because they're still children."

Doria believed Mr. Bates was gay. She wondered how much hardship or joy there had been for him in high school. "Were you popular?"

"I was very popular. I dedicated myself to popularity. Making fun of others was my specialty. I can never go to a high

62

school reunion, Doria. I'm ashamed to meet all the kids I was cruel to."

Doria didn't see a reunion in her future either. Reunions were for people who had friends.

She walked through the rain, planning the dinner conversation she would have with her parents. They always wanted to know every detail of her day, so that was what Doria would give them: details. Rebecca, she would say, was wearing the most adorable sandals, a sort of Roman gladiator look, but with wedge heels. She also shared her apple slices with me and saved me two Thin Mints.

Her parents would love that.

They would assume that Doria's whole day had been full of laughter.

***

Lutie left the lobby. Outside, she pressed the little umbrella button, enjoying the swoosh as it opened. It was a large umbrella, covered with glowing sunflowers. Way ahead, she glimpsed the tiny yellow rectangle of Doria's ugly music container.

What to do? Where to go?

If Lutie decided on Aunt Grace's, she faced a major walk west. Aunt Grace lived in one of the town-house developments that were sprinkled all over the former countryside. It had a recreation center and a swimming pool and tennis courts, the way they all did, and Aunt Grace was a serious card player, and spent many an evening slaughtering people at canasta, euchre, rummy and poker.

She watched Doria walk the other way, toward Tenth Street, which was a dividing line. North of it were patches of tough neighborhoods. South were patches of middle ground. You moved into the countryside and neighborhoods got richer and greener, with bigger houses and wider-screen TVs. Aunt Tamika and Uncle Dean lived out that way.

Either aunt would pick Lutie up after work, but that meant five-thirty at the earliest.

Lutie threaded through a long line of cars—dutiful mothers picking up sons and daughters who didn't want wet hair. Then she ran through the rain until she caught up with Doria. "Hey, Doria," she said. "You're soaked. Stand under my umbrella."

Doria was as surprised as if they had met by chance on the streets of Hong Kong. "Hi, Lutie!"

"You on your way to practice?"

Doria hoisted her yellow music case as proof.

Lutie smiled. "You can't find a music case that's not offensive to the eye?"

"Well, I know, it does look like an infected mushroom. But I don't lose it. It can't blend in. Plus other musicians—their fingers are sticky. They're not stealing or even borrowing; they just can't help cozying up to music, and the next thing you know, your teacher has all your stuff mixed in with his. But an ugly yellow case like this?" Doria shook her head. "They don't touch it."

Lutie laughed. Doria loved it when Lutie gave her wonderful hiccupping laugh.

In Doria's head, music was still composing itself, rather like the rain, notes spanging against hard surfaces. No music was as good as the sound of a friend laughing. "I'm having a music attack," she told Lutie.

"What's that like?"

"The notes gang up on me. I have to write them down or they turn on me."

"When I'm singing, it's in my head and heart and bones and down to my toes." Lutie shook herself, as if making the

64

music fall through her and land on the ground. "I have to have music escapes. Too much music and I drown."

Had Doria actually met somebody who understood her? "When you're singing," she asked Lutie, "does the music fit you, tight as the bark on a tree, and you were born with it?"

The rain stopped suddenly, as if it really had been an orchestra and the conductor had given the cue to stop. Immediately the air was hot, and the smell of sour mud and refreshed trees and oily road surface filled the air.

Lutie shook the rain off her umbrella and telescoped it into a tidy cylinder. She didn't answer, but a block later, she said, "I'm taking a class you might like. Ancient History. Mr. Amberson was telling us that the ancient Greeks saw astronomy and music as reflections of each other. Stars, planets and the moon are the visible harmony of the cosmos. Music is the invisible harmony. So, stars you stare at; music you hear."

It sounded like song lyrics. Doria wanted to share the words, text them to Nell and Steph. But they might scorn them and the words might be damaged.

Lutie began to sing a soft wordless melody that started low and then climbed, only to swoop down and swim at the bottom, where it rested like a lullaby in the middle of the day. It was haunting, like some old mountain ballad that Doria had heard in a previous life. She soaked up the notes and decided she would re-create them later on the organ.

Doria suddenly remembered the weird little conference with Mr. Gregg. *Get those songs out of Lutie. Tell her you'll play the piano for her or something.*

Is this one of the lost songs? Doria thought, dismayed. Do I have to turn it over to Mr. Gregg?

"Doria," said Lutie, "you don't really hang out in that church alone, do you?"

"Of course not," she lied.

Text messages were coming steadily now, what with school finally over and everybody needing to update everybody. Thanks to her very visible umbrella, quite a few people had seen Lutie catch up with Doria in the rain and wanted to know what was up with that. *Music,* Lutie texted back.

Miss Veola had sent a reminder. *Stop,* it said.

It occurred to Lutie that if she hauled Doria along with her, Miss Veola would behave differently. As a bonus, Doria would not be alone in the church in the dark. Maybe Lutie would get to know her better and know whether to trust her with another, more specific warning.

"What music do you listen to, Doria?" she asked. "When you're home?" Doria wasn't carrying an iPod, which Lutie would have expected.

"I don't listen to anything. I like silence. I hear music in my head. If the house is quiet, I hear better."

Lutie craved music all the time—loud and strong and room-filling. She wanted it to rock the house and make her feet dance and her skin shiver. If she ever got her own car, she'd turn up the bass on the radio so loud that at stoplights, the driver in the next lane would frown.

Lutie saw herself in all of her homes—dancing, stomping, swaying, whirling through each house and up and down all the stairs, and even on the furniture, a tap dancer in need of a platform.

She held up her cell. "My preacher wants to talk to me. She's just a few blocks down Tenth. Want to come? Miss Veola's a peach." Actually, Miss Veola was more like a pickle, sharp and briny. "She loves church music," added Lutie. "She just bought a new church and we're pretty excited about it."

66

"She bought a church?"

"An old movie theater in a dead strip mall. We're taking out the first few rows of seats to make room for a piano and an electric keyboard and a whole lot of percussion, and we also have two clarinets, a sax and a couple guitars."

Doria's eyes lit up.

Lutie propelled her around the corner, toward Miss Veola's.

⁓

When Cliff Greene was little, and he got sick, his mama took his temperature. It was an odd quiet moment, he and his mama waiting to see what the little gauge said. She had the stick kind that went under the tongue, not the forehead kind used by the nurse at the clinic.

But he wasn't Cliff anymore, and his mama didn't care what his temperature was. Train felt like the motor of his body was revved up so high that all the liquid in him had boiled off. It wasn't normal for a human, who was supposed to be ninety-eight percent water.

Used to be fun, being DeRade's shadow. Stopped being fun after Nate. Really stopped once DeRade went to prison.

Train didn't like the idea of prison.

He liked air and sky and wind and grass. At home, he had shifted the TV to the plug near the front door so he could sit outside on the porch, his tall stool tilted back to lean against the wall, and watch TV in the fresh air. That made him feel better, so he started doing it in school, too. The high school was built on one level, and most classrooms had a door to the hall plus a door to the outside. Train would walk in, shove a chair across the floor and prop the outside door open. He'd sit half in and half out of the room. Hot, cold, rain or shine— Train just sat there, ruining the heat or the air-conditioning for everybody, and think about DeRade, who wasn't going to have an open door for a long time.

The rain stopped. Kids poured out of the foyer and spread over the paving stones like pancake batter. When Train followed, they lowered their eyes, pretending to be busy. Cried, "I'll miss my bus!" and rushed away.

But when Kelvin slouched out, bringing up the rear because he was slower than mud, they all grinned. Said hey and made room for him in their group.

In kindergarten they had been the same—he and Lutie and Kelvin.

Now they were strangers.

Which reminded him of Doria, the new girl in town.

He wasn't usually attracted to keys. If you were going to break in, the fun was breaking. DeRade liked to leave a signature: a bruise, a cut or a broken window.

But there were car keys on that key chain.

Stealing cars was not what it used to be. More and more cars did not use keys, could not be hot-wired, or had LoJack or OnStar.

One had been a Honda key. Probably an old Honda, because not that many kids drove new. If he had a key, he could drive the Honda when he felt like it. If Doria drove that Honda to school, he could just take her car when he wanted fresh air.

The key chain also had a key to her house. He could open her garage when he needed wheels, and drive off. Maybe even put the car back when he was done, so he could do it again.

He saw himself coolly moving in and out of Doria's life and car and house like a ghost.

But DeRade would mock him. Ghost? he'd say. One step up from a shadow. When you gonna *do* something?

6

People new to Court Hill didn't know that Chalk existed. The word was not on any map. It was not the name of a street. It was just the name.

Miss Veola lived on the far edge of Chalk, and Lutie meant to go down Tenth Street so that she and Doria skirted the neighborhood. But she forgot and they were now squarely inside the community.

Lutie loved Chalk. She loved knowing everybody, even the bad ones. She loved the comfortable wandering from one yard to the next, the easy conversations, the always-waiting sweet tea.

But by definition, a Yankee was filled with scorn. Doria was an exception to most rules, socially, academically and musically. But Yankee would win. A Northerner expected the South to be minor league, if not outright failure. And that was what Doria Bell would see.

The houses in Chalk were so small. There was so much peeling paint. Everything sagged. Doors sagged. Screens sagged. Gutters sagged. And often, hope sagged.

No driveways, just packed earth for old cars to park on. Lanes with turns so sharp and narrow, a fire truck couldn't get through. Big trees towered above the little houses on the steep slope. Autumn leaves were bright as paint, the only color except for clothes drying on lines. On some porches men sat, half visible, drinking beer, playing cards, watching the world.

Miss Veola said that the women and children in Chalk were the best, but the men were the worst. Lutie said, "That's not Christian of you, Miss Veola. You can't write the men off like that."

"The men, they write themselves off," said Miss Veola. "If they could find Jesus, they'd see the fineness in their souls. But they're too busy finding enemies. If they don't have one, they make one."

Like Train, thought Lutie. He's not on the prowl for money or drugs. He's looking for a way to shine. Nice people are background. Violent people show up.

Maybe Saravette had broken all the commandments, but Lutie didn't think Train had. Not yet, anyway. Did he want to? Certainly DeRade had wanted to. And did. He hadn't been brought to trial for that murder, but lack of evidence didn't mean innocence in DeRade's case.

Lutie felt a stab of grief for sweet little Cliff, who had sat next to her in kindergarten. Here in Chalk, the statistics about young African American men and prison were on display, because the wide broom of crime was always sweeping.

Miss Veola refused to believe that a soul could actually be lost. She was always reaching out, by voice, food, prayer, phone, trying to wrap her fingers around the kids who were sliding away. She cared how people behaved and was always coaxing them to the Lord. When Holler went back to prison (of course his real name wasn't Holler, he was just a man who never lowered his voice, which was how the police had caught him), Miss Veola helped his babymama and the children. (Actually, she ordered Lutie to babysit.) She gave Holler a New Testament and told him to read it.

That was when they found out Holler couldn't read. Miss Veola got him on the tutor list in prison, and he was reading now. Or so he said. People lied to Miss Veola to get her off their backs.

Lutie and Doria turned a corner.

Most white people walking into Chalk would feel a shiver of concern and turn around. But the world seemed less visible to Doria than to Lutie. Lutie could imagine Doria failing to look left and right for oncoming traffic, her mind full of music. She had certainly failed to wonder about Train's motives. Whereas Lutie felt so wrapped up in the world, it was like a sweatsuit or sneakers she couldn't take off. She was zipped and laced into the world.

Miss Veola was out in her front yard, in a half circle of old plastic lawn chairs. She loved to talk, and people loved to talk with her. Little kids liked to dig through the basket she kept full of children's toys. Sitting next to Miss Veola was Miss Elminah, wearing an amazing hat. Miss Elminah was always shaded with a wide brim. She was so old she still swept her dirt front yard.

Racing around them were the little Waitlee boys, their mama sitting peaceful on her own porch next door, laughing into her cell phone.

Towering above Miss Veola's four rooms were huge oaks whose leaves just browned up and fell down, providing no autumn splendor, but could be counted on for shade through the long hot Carolina days. Beyond them was city housing—brick squares quartered into little apartments, each with its own porch. Nobody wanted the back-facing porches.

"Lutie, honey," cried Miss Elminah. "You look beautiful, darlin'. Give me some sugar." They exchanged kisses and hugs.

Lutie wondered how to introduce Doria. She could say, This is my friend.

Being friends with Doria would be like adopting a stray dog. A dog with outstanding ability and training, to be sure, but Lutie didn't want a pet, let alone one that needed as much feeding, walking and grooming as Doria. So Lutie said brightly, "This is Doria Bell, who plays the piano for concert choir and is in my AP chemistry class." Lutie always liked to throw in that Advanced Placement stuff. It was an excuse for studying, that waste of time that required a defense.

"Doria," repeated Miss Veola, in the lingering way she had with names, as if she'd been hoping somebody named Doria would come by. "Doria, I'm so glad to meet you. Have some tea, honey. Sit right down and visit with us. This is my dear friend, Miss Elminah. Miss Elminah is ninety-one years old this week."

"How do you do?" said Doria.

"And I am four!" called one of the Waitlee boys, raising fat little fingers.

Doria knelt in the wet grass beside him. "I love the number four," she confided, and the little boy understood, and they squatted there, enjoying the number four.

✺

Doria felt like a chorus member in an opera production. The curtain had closed on the stage, which had been set with fine brick mansions and prim little trees. Scene two featured grimy little houses hardly bigger than walk-in closets. Each tiny chain-linked yard had its plastic chairs and children's toys scattered under shade trees. One house had chickens.

People flowed down the street, up front steps, between

72

houses and through open, banging doors. It was like school during passing periods: everybody on their way someplace else, and everybody talking, to each other or on their cell phones, or both.

Sound splashed: conversation in every pitch, from bass men to piccolo-high babies. Music poured from car radios and boom boxes. TVs played inside houses, but who was watching? They were all outside. The choreography of their movements was the opera chorus about to gather and burst into song.

Miss Veola's house was a brown square, featuring an open front porch with two steps up and no railings. The edges were lined with potted plants, mostly orange and yellow marigolds, with a smattering of zinnias. Molded plastic chairs faced the red clay road. Each chair had a tiny table. Some of the tables were upended tins that had once held pretzels.

The four-year-old went back to his toy truck and Doria stood up. She had not developed a taste for sweet tea, or any cold tea, for that matter, but she took the glass Miss Veola offered and sipped. "Thank you," she said.

"And have a lemon bar, honey," said Miss Elminah. "I bake the best lemon bars in Court Hill."

"Probably in America," said Lutie, popping the lid off a plastic container and offering it to Doria.

Inside were little squares, very yellow, with powdered-sugar topping. Doria bit into one. It was way too sugary, but also way too tart, and the combination was delicious. It made her mouth shiver.

The two old women and Lutie chatted. They seemed to know everything there was to know about each other. The warm voices, the hot sun and the sweet tea brought Doria down. She wanted to be in another state, another town and street, where she too knew everything about everyone.

But now she couldn't even enjoy homesickness. She did not

know Nell and Steph anymore. She had only been gone three months, and already she was more of a chore to them than a friend. What if they shrugged her off as easily as they had shrugged off violin and horn?

Doria held the glass of tea to her mouth to hide her trembling chin.

Miss Elminah patted her knee. "We are so proud of our Lutie. She is just the finest student. Why, her MeeMaw, Miss Eunice, would be dancing with joy. Doria, honey, do you love school as much as Lutie does?"

How could anybody love anything without friends?

"School is fine, thank you," said Doria.

Miss Veola studied her. "Let us pray," she said.

Doria had forgotten that Miss Veola was a minister.

Miss Veola prayed upward instead of down, looking God in the eye. Doria had the feeling that there was no hiding place for the Lord when Miss Veola called his name. "Lord, you brought me a new friend," Miss Veola said.

Doria cringed. People down the block would hear.

"I love when that happens," called Miss Veola. "But Lord, I feel as if school is not good to Doria. She needs your touch. You come down to Doria, Lord. Put your arms around her. Let her feel how much she's loved."

In all the hundreds of prayers Doria had heard in church, not once had somebody named her and instructed God to be with her. Doria's reserve was melting like butter in a microwave. She clenched her stomach muscles to isolate herself from the prayer. But the prayer climbed all over her anyway.

"Amen," said Miss Veola. "And amen."

Doria felt boneless. When Miss Veola released her hand, Doria kept holding it out.

"More tea?" asked Miss Veola.

"No. I—well—it sounds silly. I was touching God."

74

"Course you were. We asked and he came." Miss Veola scooted her chair closer. Doria tried to put a mental barricade between them. "Doria, honey, I just feel your problems lying in your lap."

Doria thought of her problems as bats flying through her hair.

"You look poorly," said Miss Veola. "I feel as if you might lie awake worrying. At night, honey, you just let God take care of your problems."

"But in the morning, nothing changes!" Doria was horrified to hear herself speak. Worse, there was a witness. Lutie might tell on her.

"Maybe you didn't hand your problem over. Every evening, you just pick up that problem and give it to God. He's up all night anyway. You let him do the worrying."

Doria had to smile. "That sounds like song lyrics. *He's up all night anyway.*"

"It is a song," said Lutie.

Lutie, Miss Elminah and Miss Veola exchanged soft looks.

Lutie walked out from under the oaks and into the sunlight. She looked up at the blue sky, turned her hands over and lifted her palms as if holding a baby or presenting a gift. She breathed in so slowly that Doria had to breathe to help. Lutie threw back her head, a position from which Doria could not have sung a note.

From Lutie's throat came a low rich growl of a note, which she dragged up an octave and a half and then swirled back down, settling on a sweet warm E-flat.

She does have perfect pitch, thought Doria.

> *Mama, you sleep.*
> *All those worries—leave 'em on the porch.*
> *Set out a chair.*

God'll come by.
Mama, you sleep.

It was a lullaby, but not for the baby. It was a lullaby for the mother.

The song had no rhyme and no verses. It rocked on, going back and forth, turning itself into a chair on a porch: a chair set out for God.

And God was there.

Rocking.

Lutie let go of the song. Lowered her hands. Sat.

"I don't know why I'm crying," said Doria, accepting a tissue from Miss Elminah.

"Because God came," said Miss Veola. "He's on the porch. You left him your worries and he took them." She took Doria's hand in hers, and Miss Elminah took Doria's other hand. Lutie finished the circle and Miss Veola prayed once more. "Jesus, all your daughters need you. Your daughter Doria, she needs you. She's got an ache she's keeping to herself. You heal that ache, Lord, because this child of yours doesn't need it. You guide her steps. And Lord, Miss Elminah needs you. She doesn't hear from her grandchildren and her heart is broken. She's never even seen her two great-grandchildren, they're so far away in miles and in love. You fix that, Lord. It needs fixing. And your lost daughter Saravette, guide her steps. Keep her from harm, and keep her from harming others. And your child Lutie, O Lord, guide her steps. Let Lutie remember all the strong women in her family, all they gave her and all she can give back. In the name of Jesus. Amen."

Doria sat inside the prayer, adding a few lines. Lord, what about Nell and Steph? I want them to miss me! I want to have left a hole in their lives! I want them to care what I'm doing.

76

When she looked up, Lutie was glaring at Miss Veola. Miss Veola was glaring right back.

Doria did not want them to argue. She did not want to know what the glares meant. "Miss Veola?" she said, rather proud of using this Southern form of address.

"Ma'am?"

A Southern-style answer. Doria was sixteen, and here was this woman of sixty—maybe even seventy or eighty; who could tell?—calling her ma'am. They did that in the South. The checker in the grocery store, the lawyer at the closing—yes, ma'am, they all said.

Doria offered a new subject. "In your prayer, you kept saying 'guide her steps.' Isn't that a church anthem?"

"The one I know is 'order my steps.' I love that one!" said Miss Veola. "I love to give orders. In another life, I might have become an army officer, so I could have a platoon or a battalion to order around. Well, the trouble with giving orders is, people don't even want suggestions. In Chalk, if you don't get your education in the schools, you'll get it in the streets. Only half our boys will finish high school. I cannot order them to stay in school. I cannot order them to be righteous. I can only remind them that God will be with them, holding their hands, if they ask him."

"Why do they have to ask? Why doesn't God just do that anyway, if he loves them?"

"Oh, Doria, that's one of the big questions. Why doesn't he? I do not know."

Train's house sat high on the hill of Chalk.

He tilted his head back, smoking and watching the world go by. He loved cigarettes. He wouldn't mind a life where nothing ever happened except his long legs dangling and smoke filling his lungs.

When he heard Lutie sing, he stood on the porch rail to get another three feet of height. Over roofs and branches he could see part of Miss Veola's yard.

He didn't remember Lutie's grandmother singing this slow sweet song. He mostly remembered when old Miz Painter shouted at God. That woman had been a truant officer, accusing God of absenteeism.

Train considered parading past Miss Veola's to prove that she lost more kids than she won. But Veola Mixton was the worst do-gooder he knew, and Train had been forced to deal with a lot of do-gooders. She'd barrel out and try to get him to visit. She'd offer sweet tea or macaroni and cheese (she did make the best mac and cheese in the world, with bacon all through it and crushed potato chips on top; and shove it under the broiler at the end, so that it came out crusty and perfect.) But quick, she'd head to prayer.

Train had lived with praying people all his life.

He knew the power of prayer. It could grab the most surprising people. What it did was, it lowered your resistance. It was a virus, hard to shake.

His mama never missed church and had dragged DeRade until he got too big. Dragged Train until Train got too big. She gave up. In school, people had given up on Train too. They were waiting for him to drop out and go away so they'd be free.

But it wasn't really prayer that made Train wary of Miss Veola. It was remembering who he had been when he was little.

Kelvin and Lutie, they were still like the little kids they had been.

Course, Kelvin never lived in Chalk. His daddy went into

78

the army, got college degrees, and now had a fine job, and Kelvin never lived anywhere but one of those show-offy neighborhoods. His family showed off every time they came to Miss Veola's church. Just showing up was showing off. And what did Kelvin ever do but sit there getting fatter?

And Lutie—the prettiest girl he would ever see, who sparkled like soda, all bubbles and clear ginger-ale excitement—Lutie had never really lived in Chalk either. Old Miz Painter's house was on the other side of Peter Creek, which Train would cross during drought, when it was only a trickle, but not the rest of the year, when the underbrush shivered and spoke with the sound of little animals, and he could feel snakes watching.

When her MeeMaw died, Lutie had gone to stay with an aunt, some woman who wouldn't lower herself going to Miss Veola's church. Probably went uptown, to some sleek rich place.

Lutie and Kelvin weren't afraid of him, but they didn't think much of him. He needed people to be afraid of him. See the heat rising off him and be scared. If they weren't actually afraid, like they were of DeRade, then Train was just noise.

Was that Doria under the oak? He'd been asking about Doria all afternoon. Got plenty of texts but not much detail.

Had Lutie really adopted her? People were saying that. Train didn't believe it. Lutie liked people who were sharp as tacks, and Doria was dumber than dirt.

He heard Miss Veola praying in her big braying voice, like God was deaf.

Train went back to his stool and turned up the volume on the TV. Drown that out.

Usually he watched sports, but today he had turned to a news channel because yet another married politician had got caught cheating with sexy girlfriends and he wanted to check them out. Instead they showed a kid who had refused to pay some friends the forty dollars he owed them. The friends doused him with alcohol and flicked a cigarette lighter at him.

They didn't show the burned kid, who was now in a special burn ward in a special burn hospital, without any skin left. They showed the kids who'd done it, young and skinny and white and crying and even slobbering, claiming they hadn't realized the victim would actually catch fire and that his skin would burn off.

Train lit another cigarette. He studied the flame at the end of his plastic lighter.

The kid had probably been annoyed when his friends threw liquid at him. Probably wondered what it was. Let's see. Not Pepsi . . . not water . . .

And all of a sudden—flames. The kid probably didn't remember elementary school safety class: stop, drop and roll. Probably not easy to remember if you were actually on fire.

Train imagined the victim running, fire eating his face. And when the victim screamed, fire leaning down his throat.

He imagined the friends chest-bumping.

Miss Veola had asked God to keep Saravette from harming others. So Miss Veola knew, or guessed, that Saravette had harmed others in the past. Lutie could ask for details. But did she want the answer?

Miss Elminah leaned forward, her dark wrinkled face full of nostalgia and pleasure. "Lutie, honey, I been remembering the ironing song. The one where you ain't got no sword. Remember that one? Sing me that one."

Who alive today could imagine the life her great-great-grandmother Mabel Painter had led? Lutie knew sweat; everybody in the Carolinas knew sweat, and she had seen people scraping by on a few dollars. But at Aunt Tamika and Uncle

Dean's, there was no scraping. There was only splurging. Mabel Painter's life had been without cell phones, electricity, even running water when she'd earned her living as a laundress. Mabel Painter would have been respected in Chalk, but beyond its invisible borders, she too would have been invisible.

Lutie didn't want to sing the ironing song. It was a song about failure. MeeMaw used to sing it in the dark, when her heart was sore and nothing helped. Lutie had to get out of here. "Maybe another time, Miss Elminah. But right now, Doria has to leave."

"No, no," said Doria. "Don't hurry on my account."

Lutie wanted to kick her.

"Please?" said Miss Elminah. "I don't think I have heard that one since your MeeMaw stood on her porch and begged God."

My grandmother never begged for anything in her life, thought Lutie. She was praying. MeeMaw handed her heart to God and I don't think he was as grateful as he should have been.

Miss Veola lowered her head, like a rhinoceros about to charge. Lutie had no choice. If Miss Elminah's own grandchildren couldn't bother with her, Lutie had to.

Fine. She would let the Lord have it. She would throw the anguish of the day in his face.

Lutie sang the ironing song.

> *"Ain't got no sword.*
> *Got just a ironing board.*
> *Can't fight for you, Lord.*
> *But show me where to stand, Lord.*
> *Want to make life here grand, Lord.*
>
> *"Got baskets of clothes to fold.*
> *Feeling old, Lord, feeling old.*

Lord, I done give all I got to give.
Don't have to iron up where you live.
I'm too tired to stand, Lord.
Don't care if life's grand, Lord.

"Take me home, Lord.
Take me home."

⌒

Kelvin's daddy had grown up in Chalk, but Kelvin lived in an impressive subdivision a mile and a world away. Kelvin walked down Tenth Street, headed home after a nice afternoon of watching other people play sports.

Kelvin too had received a text from Miss Veola. *Stop.*

Miss Veola was concerned that Kelvin was throwing away the brains, ability and future that God had given him. She was bound to place a demand that Kelvin wouldn't want to fulfill, but then, so did everybody. Kelvin was used to it. No, the hard part of a visit with Miss Veola was that his parents only went to her church some of the time. Miss Veola's service lasted too long. She preached and preached. She could have fifty scripture references, and wait for the congregation to find each verse in their own Bibles. Kelvin's father preferred a speedier service, with speedy hymns, speedy prayers and a nice short message. Kelvin's mother mainly loved coffee hour so she could chat with her girlfriends, and she usually ducked out before the sermon, claiming she had to cut sandwiches into little triangles.

Kelvin approached Miss Veola's house from the side. Beyond the thick trunks of oaks and the fat green sprawl of untrimmed azaleas, he could see that Miss Veola had visitors. This was good. She was busy. Kelvin could say "hey," and leave.

Since Miss Veola was in the middle of a prayer, Kelvin leaned against an oak, waiting for the prayer to end before he walked up.

Prayer didn't bother Kelvin one way or another. He was touched when people seemed to believe that a prayer went somewhere. But he saw no evidence that it did or ever had. He remembered way back, maybe first or second grade, when he and Cliff Greene had wanted to be preachers. They used to pile crates up to use as a pulpit and shout "Amen!" That version of Cliff had vanished and there was no sign that it would ever return.

Miss Veola's prayer shocked Kelvin. He had not known that Miss Elminah had been discarded by her distant grandchildren, that they couldn't even be bothered to bring their babies to meet her. He would tell his mother, who would come visit Miss Elminah.

He did not know the name Saravette, but she was obviously a problem.

Wait—Miss Veola was praying for Doria? Doria Bell? Doria was in Miss Veola's yard too?

He laughed at the idea that Doria needed God to guide her steps. Of course, Doria could use a little help in the social category, but she would grow into herself. There would come a day when Kelvin would brag: I was in school with her.

Then Lutie began to sing, her voice a cloud floating in heaven.

He did not know the song, but it had to be from the Laundry List. Those pieces were distinctive. His daddy talked about it now and then. "Old Miz Painter," he'd say, meaning Lutie's MeeMaw. "She was a piece of work. She'd sit on that little porch of hers, singing and singing. Her voice would carry over the fields and through the woods. She talked to the Lord like he was her teenage son and she had to bring him into line. We used to wait for lightning to strike."

This was not one of those songs.

It was a lament, with legs too tired to stand.

Until the end.

Then the song became rich with belief and glad with waiting. "Take me home, Lord," said the song, absolutely sure that the Lord was on his way.

Doria did not have to hear music twice to have it in her memory. She had heard three of Lutie's songs now and as soon as she was at her computer, she'd write them down. On the first pass, she'd write exactly what Lutie had sung: a line of notes, hanging below heaven. On the second pass, she'd add her own choice of chords. Just something for the songs to stand on.

Lutie's voice soared out of the little yard, up into the wind. She was visibly connected to God, her hands stretching to reach his.

There has to be a video, thought Doria. Right here. Just like this. These are the songs Mr. Gregg wants. He's never heard them. He doesn't know for sure that they even exist.

But they do.

And he's right.

Whoever owns these has a ticket out.

Lutie had a trembly feeling from being so close to God. Like people in the Old Testament who had to hide their faces from him or go up in smoke.

"Lutie, what a range you have," marveled Doria. "And what a melody. I feel as if I've been waiting inside myself to hear that."

Lutie was exhausted. She wanted to sweep everybody away,

including Mabel Painter. She said dismissively, "My grand-mother's grandmother wrote quite a few songs. I don't sing them often. I can't sing them for just anybody."

Doria got flustered and looked away.

Lutie was sick of her. Why am I bothering with this limp excuse for a person? She's your problem, God. I'm leaving her on a porch somewhere. Take her away.

Miss Elminah said, "Sing another one, honey bunny."

"I'm done," said Lutie sharply. "Those songs are too much. I can't do them all in a row."

"Lutie, do not be a prima donna," said Miss Veola. "You are perfectly capable of singing all of them in a row, and your MeeMaw used to do just that, with you beside her. You are being difficult and mean."

Lutie glared at her.

"You know the plans for our new church!" cried Miss Veola. "It will cost and cost. You could give a concert that would bring in people from all over the Carolinas."

God was gone, if he had ever been here. No prayer stretched to the sky. Religion was nothing but a spell that had been broken.

"The Laundry List doesn't belong to them and it doesn't belong to you," snapped Lutie. "Come on, Doria. We have to go."

Doria turned to follow.

Standing by the fence that surrounded the little yard was Kelvin. Low rays of sun caught his dark skin, making him glow. Doria's heart turned over. She wanted to touch him, to touch his arm and his hand, his cheek and his hair.

She wanted him to touch her.

"Hey, Doria," he said, easy as summer, as if Doria hanging out in a rural slum in a black preacher's yard were perfectly ordinary.

"Hi, Kelvin." She loved saying his name. The "l" was fat and soft in her mouth, followed by that vibrating "v" and the half-humming "n."

But he had already turned to Lutie. "Hey, Lutie. Heard you sing. It was beautiful."

For a moment, there was no Miss Veola, no Miss Elminah, no little Waitlee boys racing around the yard. There was only Lutie, beautiful to Kelvin—and Kelvin, beautiful to Lutie.

"Thanks for that wonderful music, Lutie," said Doria stiffly. "Thank you for tea, Miss Veola. Thank you for the lemon bar, Miss Elminah. I'll be heading on." She would practice. Practice lining up her fingers, her feet and her mind.

Doria turned her back, took one step and lost the lovely touch of God.

Her parents disapproved of emotional religion and now she saw why. You needed to keep things on a low level. You could not get overly involved with God. You should not get overly involved at school either. You'd always be in a state of want— wanting heavenly attention, wanting friends, wanting a boyfriend . . . wanting Kelvin. But you wouldn't have them.

If you stood at a distance, though, at least you could enjoy what you did have, like music.

"I'll head back with you, Doria," said Lutie. "Doria's going to practice the organ at her church and I'm going to Aunt Grace's," she explained to everyone.

"Sweet," said Kelvin.

How smooth his face was. How much Doria wanted to touch it.

"Doria," he said, "somebody told me you practice every single day at First Methodist. Is that true?"

This felt like something Doria should not agree with. Popular kids did not practice the organ every single day. "Church is where the organs are," she said lightly. "Can't practice at the gym."

"If you're alone, it's a bad idea."

They were all so annoying. Who exactly did they think was willing to sit on a pew for two hours every day while she practiced? "I'm not alone, Kelvin," she lied.

"Just one moment, Miss Lutie," said Miss Veola sharply. "What is your explanation for missing half a day of school?"

"None of your business," said Lutie. "Hurry up, Doria."

Doria could not imagine anybody being rude to Miss Veola. From Kelvin's expression, he couldn't imagine it either. Miss Veola *really* couldn't believe it. But the pastor rallied. "Now don't be a stranger, Doria," she said.

Except I am a stranger, thought Doria. And now even my old friends Nell and Stephanie are strangers.

When Train brought DeRade the barbed wire he'd been ordered to cut, DeRade explained that he would truss Nate up like they did in cartoons, and Nate would have to inch down the street with his arms pinned to his sides, shivering and crying inside the wire. People would stare, laugh and unwrap him.

But it hadn't worked out that way, or else DeRade had been lying when he'd described the plan. Nate had flailed around, screaming and jerking, and put out his eye all by himself.

Some nights Train was blind in one eye, too. Some nights it was his body that flailed and jerked.

Now Train was on fire thinking about that kid on fire.

Down the road, Lutie was singing another song from the Laundry List. Train left his house. Behind him the TV kept blaring. He worked his way across the path that wandered along the top of the hill, behind the row of little houses, until he was above Miss Veola's.

Kelvin was there. Kelvin, who had become a fat jerk who did nothing but sprawl on chairs and laugh. On whom teachers doted. Nobody wrote Kelvin off just because he did nothing. They embraced him.

Lutie and Doria were beaming at Kelvin, and so were Miss Veola and Miss Elminah.

The terrible heat coursed through Train. He felt as if he, too, had been doused with alcohol and set on fire. He hated them for being soft and happy and stupid and successful.

He didn't know which one made him the craziest.

But he did know the easiest one to hurt.

7

Lutie stalked back to Tenth Street.

All these prayers, all this demand for song, all these plans for her future, Lutie could imagine it ending in disaster. Miss Veola would scoop Saravette up and throw her back in Lutie's life, complete with lice and crystal meth and soiled sweaters. Saravette would contaminate the landscape of Lutie's life.

She was trotting. Doria was panting to keep up. They reached the corner of Tenth and Hill. In the bushes beside the road, a mockingbird burst into song. It trilled wildly, as if it might run out of time and had to condense a life of song into a minute.

Lutie could see the First Methodist church spire. She didn't have to walk any farther, just give Doria a push. She didn't have any courtesy left. She didn't like herself for being rude to Miss Veola, but the pastor kept cornering her. How many times did Lutie have to say no?

Doria said, "Thank you for a nice afternoon, Lutie. And thank you so much for the songs. I will cherish them."

Why couldn't Doria talk like a normal person? She sounded like a greeting card.

Lutie checked her messages. It looked as if people had accepted the music excuse for why she was with Doria, because nobody asked in their second text. But now Aunt Grace was on her case. It was fine for Lutie to communicate with everybody instantly, but totally annoying when the various severe ladies in her life did it. Skipping school felt like a hundred years ago.

"Mr. Gregg asked me to do something," said Doria timidly.

Lutie hated timid people.

Doria wet her lips.

Lutie hated people who had to dampen their lips before they spoke.

"When he texted, we were at lunch, and Rebecca thought Mr. Gregg wanted to talk about his musical," said Doria.

For years Mr. Gregg had been claiming to be almost done writing his musical. Lutie wasn't sure there really was one. She thought it was more daydream than reality, and that broke her heart, because she loved Mr. Gregg.

"But in fact, Mr. Gregg asked me to get some family songs out of you, Lutie. He called them the Laundry List. When he saw you take me to lunch, he figured you'd give me your songs because of our friendship."

The mockingbird was chirping wildly now, crazed with song. Lutie felt the same. How dare these greedy needy people trespass on her?

"I told him that you and I are not friends," said Doria. "You're just being kind."

It was too true for eye contact. Lutie looked away.

"Those were the songs, weren't they?"

Lutie shrugged.

"They are a treasure, Lutie. All the singing world would love to hear them. And learn them. And lean on them."

"You selling me out?" she demanded.

"No," said Doria, her voice solid and quiet.

I should give her a chance, thought Lutie. But it's a shot in a hundred and I like better odds.

"Sometimes when I play Bach, Lutie, I think of the millions of people who have cherished Bach's music. Hundreds of millions, I suppose, if you're thinking of, say, 'Jesu, Joy of Man's Desiring.' Over the centuries and throughout the world."

Lutie wondered if Mabel Painter had ever heard Baroque music. Or any recorded music, for that matter. Had she been alive when record players were invented? When did radio begin? Lutie didn't even know the dates of her great-great-grandmother's life. She could ask Professor Durham. He would know.

Which offended Lutie. She said sharply, "So my great-great-grandmother's music also belongs to hundreds of millions of people, and I need to give it away?"

Doria smiled. How beautiful her smile was. Transforming. "The last thing you should do is give those songs away. But you should perform them. Lutie, I can just see you on the stage of that new church, facing a thousand people who paid a lot to get in, and every one of them excited about being the very first audience to hear the lost songs of a lost time. I see you in some long spangled gown, walking out on that stage, a spotlight wrapping you in dazzle. Lutie, you would own any stage you walked on. I see the audience starting out skeptical, expecting little basic tunes that sound like any other basic tunes. Expecting an ordinary voice. And they'll get you. And they'll get Mabel Painter, shouting to God. And their skin will prickle and there will be tears in their eyes."

Lutie's skin prickled. She got tears in her eyes.

After a while, Doria said, "Would it be okay with you if I wrote those songs down?"

Lutie was sorry she had walked one step with Doria Bell, never mind a mile. The idea that a skinny loser Yankee white girl dared ask for the music of Mabel Painter made Lutie want to stomp her. "They aren't songs. They're prayers. They just happen to have melodies. Don't call them property. They're beyond that. They're half heaven. No, you can't write them down."

Lutie suppressed a shudder. If she had to sing the whole list, all in a row, there would be side effects. Lutie would teeter on the precipice of some dark century and have the hideous sensation of becoming Mabel, with Mabel's endless labor and aching back. Mabel Painter had been close to slavery, and Lutie hated thinking about that grim slab of history. Sometimes when she read about it—or sang about it—she'd feel shackles on her ankles, feel herself being seized. Shipped. Sold. Becoming property. No different from a cow or a couch.

If she became known for the Laundry List, it would be a chain binding her to Mabel. Lutie figured she had enough chains, being bound to Saravette. Because that was another side effect to presenting the Laundry List. Saravette might come.

"I play a lot of Bach on the organ," said Doria, "and of course he's all God, all the time, but I don't think of his works as prayer. Bach honors God, but his music doesn't actually address God. You, though, you had to walk out under the sky and get visible, and talk to God with nothing in your way."

Doria gripped a subject as tight as Miss Veola did. They both seemed to think in straight lines, like fishing poles: reeling in thoughts, neatly winding them. Lutie's thoughts were individuals; in fact, like laundry. Some damp, some dry, some folded, some dirty. Making sense of them would be a long hot task with a heavy iron. "What would you do with my songs if you wrote them down? Hand them to Mr. Gregg? Try to make money off them?"

"Oh, no. It's more that I feel them in my fingers. I need to pour the notes onto the keyboard and then I need to attach them to the page." She held up her hands, fingers curved, as if she were about to play.

"But they're not yours! Here's what Mabel Painter said to her granddaughter, my MeeMaw. 'They can bring me their baskets of soiled clothes. I will scrub and starch and hang them up to dry. I will iron and sweat and earn nickels and dimes. I will be proud of how clean and smooth the laundry is. All the day long, to all the world, I will be nobody. And at the end of the day, I will sing. And when I sing, I, Mabel Painter, am a child of God. When I sing, he listens.'"

Doria closed her eyes. "'I, Mabel Painter, am a child of God,'" she whispered. "'When I sing, he listens.'"

Lutie had had enough. "Yeah. Whatever. You know where you are now? See the steeple?"

In a moment, Doria was alone on the cracked sidewalk. Her heart ached enough that she could have taken a Tylenol. She didn't have the energy to push the Walk button.

Lord, I done give all I got to give, she thought. Don't have to go friendless to school up where you live. Take me home, Lord.

But away from Miss Veola, who was a tree trunk of certainty, Doria did not believe that she could set a chair on her porch and God would come by.

Doria had self-discipline. She needed it now. She removed pointless self-pity from her mind and inserted the Bach fugue she was learning. Bach was particularly space taking. In her mind, she usually felt Bach inside out and upside down, from left to right and top to bottom. But not this time. Self-discipline was not there.

She was just a loser standing on a corner, watching the world go by.

If her mother and father knew she felt this way, they would be destroyed. They believed she had a good life, full of friends and achievements and activities. I should have told them more, she thought. I wouldn't know where to start now.

A storm was rolling in from the west, curling black and purple. The heat of the day had vanished, flattened by the coming change in the weather. Doria felt flattened too.

From behind her a man's voice said, "Hey, Miss Doria."

She was so startled that her body jerked and she whirled around. The man was tall and her eyes first met his T-shirt. She had to drag her gaze upward.

It was Train.

Train was handsome, a different brown from Kelvin or Lutie, more bronze. All of him was thin—face, mouth, body, hands. His hair was wild, half caught in a rag; his clothing mismatched and too large. He looked the way she felt. "Hello, Train," she said.

"You going to practice at your church?"

How did people know so much about her? Doria never talked to anybody. Why would people bother to share such useless information? "I usually do, but I think it's too late." Although normally it was never too late for music. Normally it was always the right time for Bach. But right now, Doria felt as if something vital had broken inside her.

"What you practice for?"

"I'm a church organist. I have a lot to play every Sunday." She was sick of admitting this. It had begun to sound vaguely criminal. "When I'm done with all the music I need for the service, then I practice music I actually want to play, which is hardly ever the same thing."

He nodded. "How I feel about Music Appreciation."

She had to laugh. "Why are you taking it, anyway?"

"Can't remember."

Talking to somebody was better than Tylenol. She wanted to keep talking. She had only one real topic, so she used it. "I just heard some new music. Beautiful music. You know Lutie, don't you?"

"Everybody knows Lutie."

How affectionate he sounded. How did Lutie do it? Lutie didn't have to worry about making friends. She just had them. If they weren't her friends in the morning, they'd be friends by afternoon. Doria was exhausted again. "Right. Well, just now, Lutie sang three songs."

"I heard."

"You did?"

"I live just up from Miss Veola. I was on my porch."

"Doesn't Lutie have the most amazing voice in the whole wide world? And those songs! Her great-great-grandmother's songs. I don't know what category to put them in."

"Category?"

"Well, for example, they aren't rap."

Train laughed. He seemed surprised by the sound of his own laugh and the stretch of his own mouth. "Not rap," he agreed. "Not Renaissance either."

"Train, you so do not look like a person who is into Renaissance music."

"I'm not. Mr. Gregg is. It was a long week listening to that."

They were both laughing now.

"Lutie sing the songs for you?" he asked.

"I think she sang them for God. Or Miss Veola."

"They sort of the same," said Train.

"I know what you mean. You know what? She prayed for me. Miss Veola."

Train nodded. It occurred to Doria that if he had heard Lutie sing, he had heard Miss Veola pray. "I never had anybody pray just for me, holding my hand," she told him. "Most prayers are group activities. You sit on the pew, the pastor talks to God, you all say amen. With Miss Veola, it was more of—well—I'm not sure what it was more of . . . I'm still thinking."

"You let me know," said Train.

People rarely meant what they said, especially in this courteous part of the world. Not even Miss Veola meant it when she used that Southern expression—Don't be a stranger. It was just a way of saying good-bye. But Doria thought that Train really did want to know what Miss Veola's prayer had been.

A school bus was approaching from the direction of the high school. Doria looked at the time. Four fifty-five. The late bus, packed with kids whose team practice or games were over.

The bus honked. Its stuttering red lights came on and a stop sign popped out. A boy who lived on Doria's street, which was miles from here, got off. Perhaps he had a dentist's appointment in the medical building behind them. Pierce Andrews was his name. He and Doria sometimes stood together at the bus stop in the morning but rarely spoke. Pierce was the handsome smooth blond type who seemed impenetrable, as if he were glazed, like pottery. When he didn't bother to speak to her in the morning, it started the whole school day in defeat.

"Hey, Doria!" yelled Pierce. "We stopped for you! Come on, get a ride home!"

Pierce had gotten the driver to make an irregular stop? How extraordinary. She would have said Pierce might not even recognize her out of context. "It was nice talking to you, Train," she told him. "I will let you know if I figure Miss Veola out."

Train said nothing. She waited, but his face said nothing either. He did not seem to occupy his face at this moment. It was empty. He was empty.

She was suddenly afraid of him; afraid of standing there; afraid of the storm about to break. She hurried across the street. "Pierce, that was so thoughtful of you." She climbed on the bus and he got on after her, and the driver pulled the doors shut.

"Wasn't me. Azure Lee said to stop."

Azure Lee Smith lived next door to Pierce, a dozen houses beyond Doria on the same road. Azure Lee was a senior, so good at basketball that she was being courted by colleges. Doria had always meant to go to a basketball game but there was never time. Well, truthfully, there was never anybody to sit with. She followed Pierce to the middle of the bus, where Azure Lee patted the seat beside her.

At the bus stop, Azure Lee always said good morning to Doria, but not in a voice that encouraged discussion. Doria sat down uncertainly. Next to Azure Lee, she felt like a pencil. Far darker than Lutie or Kelvin or Train, Azure Lee was also taller and stronger than any of them. She was beautiful in a sports warrior kind of way.

"Shove over," said Pierce, cramming himself into the two-person bench next to Doria.

"I took one look at you," Azure Lee told Doria, "and I yelled to the bus driver, 'We are picking that girl up!'"

Doria was mystified.

"Train," explained Azure Lee. "That boy is going off his tracks. You don't need to mix it up with him."

"Is Train his real name?"

"Cliff is his real name," said Pierce. "We were in elementary school together. But he's got a killer older brother. Probably a matter of hours before Train is too."

Doria misunderstood the adjective *killer*. "He is very good-looking," she agreed.

"No," said Azure Lee irritably. "His older brother probably did kill somebody a few years ago. But they didn't get DeRade for that. They got him for blinding a kid."

Doria was horrified. What would life be like if you were blind? How would you read music or books? "But I liked Train," she protested. "We were chatting about music."

Azure Lee shook her head. "Sounds like you. But he's falling apart. You don't want to be there when it happens."

The bus reached their subdivision, Fountain Ridge. It had no fountains and no ridges. The three of them got off. She felt Pierce's height and Azure Lee's strength. Walking between them was like having an armed escort.

"I heard a rumor that Train wanted your key ring," said Pierce. "Train is seriously bad news. Was he asking about your keys, Doria? There on the corner?"

"No."

"And you have your keys? He didn't steal them?"

Doria was offended. She was careful with her keys. Pierce and Azure Lee were exaggerating. "I thought he was charming," she said stiffly.

"He probably was. But it's just a tool for him. He wouldn't waste his time on you if he wasn't working an angle."

Mr. Gregg's angle was to get the Laundry List. Jenny's

angle was to get the solo. Lutie's angle was to add to her kindness list. There wasn't anybody who just wanted to hang out with Doria. Why should Train be different?

"Listen," said Pierce, "my dad's a detective in the police force. Everything around here looks nice, but there are tough neighborhoods that somebody like you would never stumble on. Train lives in one. It's called Chalk."

Doria had seen Chalk. The debris and poverty. The lounging men, silent and staring.

And she had heard Chalk. The prayers, the clinking of ice in glasses of tea, the laughter of four-year-olds and the songs to God.

She looked sideways at Pierce, to see if she could share any of this, but she could read nothing in his profile.

Fountain Ridge had one long street with seven short cul-de-sacs, and four house styles. The developer had planted three kinds of trees and two varieties of hedge. All the crape myrtles bloomed at the same time in the same color. All the street maples turned wine-red the same day in the fall. The neighborhood had a prim clean look, like educational toys.

Doria's house was closest.

Pierce said, "I don't see why Train would be interested in your keys unless he's interested in your house. Anybody home right now? Your parents?"

"They both work. Nobody's home yet."

Azure Lee, Pierce and Doria lived in the exact same house, except that Azure Lee's was flipped and Pierce's had a walk-out basement. They walked carefully up her driveway with her, as if Train might be lurking in the bushes. Doria put her key into each lock. The alarm chirped. She stepped in and silenced it. In every house, the control panel was just inside the door.

Doria took them on a tour so they could see what

extra-cost options had been put in the kitchen and how their window treatments compared.

"Doria, your house is beautiful," said Pierce. "It's so different from ours. My parents are IKEA people. We're always going up there and finding something new."

"I want to cuddle up on all these great chairs and sofas," agreed Azure Lee.

"It's kind of a sanctuary for me," said Doria, and immediately regretted her choice of word.

"People who need a sanctuary are on the run from something," said Pierce. "They gotta hide in a safe place." He was smiling at her, and it was a warm soft smile, the kind anybody would want directed at them, but Doria was shocked. Was she on the run? Hiding? Was life on the piano bench actually a sanctuary from other kids?

If so, she had to quit sitting on benches. She had to move into groups, into the middle, among friends.

"You're trying out all the chairs, Azure Lee. Like the three bears," teased Pierce. Then his voice changed. "What is this?"

"A physics textbook," said Doria.

"You're not in physics," said Pierce, who was.

"No. I couldn't fit it into my schedule."

"So you're doing it on your own?"

"Well, kind of. I'm taking an online course."

She watched their faces as they mentally clicked through what they knew of her schedule: precalc, honors chemistry, honors English, third-year Spanish, music composition . . . and for fun, physics in her spare time at home.

Pierce and Azure Lee practically tripped over each other getting to the door.

It was fine for Azure Lee to go beyond the boundaries in basketball. Everybody loved that she spent hours every day in her driveway, her only company the net above her garage door. Everybody loved her ambition to become a pro. But a thirst for knowledge was not the same. If you went beyond the boundaries there, you were exiled.

Azure Lee reached the safety of the front entrance. "Doria, with your grades and all this stuff you do on the side, you could probably skip senior year, graduate with Pierce and me in May and go straight to college."

"Pick a big school," added Pierce, "where they have everything."

Azure Lee and Pierce reached the sidewalk. They exchanged glances, but not with Doria.

For a long time after the late bus disappeared, Train stood by the side of the road, immobilized. Prissy pale Pierce had made a school bus stop in order to remove Doria from Train's presence.

It was several minutes before Train remembered that this was what he wanted: to be feared.

He received a text.

Stop.

It was from Miss Veola, of course. Woman didn't know when she was beaten.

Train deleted it.

Aunt Grace's text said, *Spend the night with me?*

Lutie almost always spent school nights at Aunt Tamika's. Perhaps Aunt Grace had been delegated to tan Lutie's hide for cutting school.

Aunt Grace lived on the other side of town. Two malls, two parks, another high school, a bunch of factories and nine miles away. Lutie texted that she'd wait at the library until Aunt Grace picked her up. Wouldn't be a long wait. They'd killed a lot of time at Miss Veola's.

Aunt Grace ran the local Department of Motor Vehicles, the only completely courteous DMV in the nation. The employees were polite to the public because they were afraid of Aunt Grace, not because she set a good example. Aunt Grace did not smile; she intimidated. When Lutie stayed with her, they sat silently at the kitchen table, Aunt Grace staring while Lutie did homework. If Lutie closed her books and said she was done, Aunt Grace would say, "Study is never done. It isn't bedtime yet. Keep at it. This is your ticket out."

A ticket out. That was what you were supposed to want if you lived in Chalk.

Yet in the laundry songs, Mabel Painter never asked for a ticket out. She asked for a way to make her own place grand. She wanted the Lord to show up in her front yard and rock on her porch.

And had he? Silently, Lutie worked her way through the songs, to see if there was one that celebrated the day the Lord showed up. At the edge of her mind a few notes wavered and a bit of melody teetered. She tried to float on the scraps of music and remember the rest of it.

It wouldn't quite come back to her.

Lost songs, Mr. Gregg and Professor Durham had called them. And sure enough, she had lost one.

It was disturbing. Lutie was the keeper of these songs, not the loser. They do have to be written down, she thought. Or recorded. I do have to cooperate with somebody, somewhere.

She had seldom been in a less cooperative mood.

She went outside the library to wait for her aunt. Then the storm came. Lutie sheltered under the overhang and watched the lightning. A few more notes came to mind, and some of the words.

Be you still alive?
Or be you still forever?

Doria Bell never cried. It gave her a headache and accomplished nothing. She stood in her silent house, refusing to give in to the desire to weep. Her best shot at friends, two beautiful people who lived on the same street, and she had owned up to being a nutcase who studied physics for fun.

And then she heard what Azure Lee had said: *graduate early.*

Court Hill can be temporary! she thought. I don't have to worry about making friends! I'm just marking time here. It's the first week in November. School ends in May. Seven more months and Court Hill can be history.

Doria picked up the TV remote and surfed the music channels. Dance came into her feet, like a pedal part on the organ, and she danced into the kitchen, around the island and through the pantry, circled the dining table and shifted into the sunroom.

College would save her. At college, she would find exclusively kids who loved to learn.

Well, of course, Stephanie's older brother and sister were now in college, where they made friends only with kids who loved to drink, party and skip class. And they were at colleges famous for academics. So even at college, Doria would have to hunt around. Pierce was right. Pick a big school. Forty thousand students, say. If five percent were as driven as Doria, she'd have two thousand to choose from.

"Holy smoke," said her father, coming in the garage door.

"Pop Latino? Did *you* put that on?" He had bought Chinese. He set little white boxes with rich scents and strong sauces all over the kitchen counter.

Mom was right behind him. She checked out the video on the TV screen. "Did it come on by itself? Do we have a glitch? Or did our actual biological daughter put it on?"

"Research," said Doria.

"Do I believe that?" said her father. "Or are you undergoing a personality change? Doria, you are sparkling. Something great happened, huh?"

Her mother was already separating chopsticks. Her father was already squishing rice onto his plate. Her parents came home starving, like little kids after school. Now she really wanted to weep, seeing them wash their hands at top speed, throw dishes onto place mats, shove glasses under the crushed-ice spout in the freezer door, and drop into their chairs.

A family is a specialized calendar: birthdays, landmarks, school years, Christmases, graduations. Drop a year? Just let it fall out of the family plan? Not graduate with her own class? Abandon her parents in a town and a state she barely knew? Go have her own life, whatever that was?

A year they had all counted on, without even knowing it. Her senior year. Lost.

Graduating early would be a door slammed in her parents' faces.

Doria told her parents about Miss Veola instead. Miss Elminah. The four-year-old and the glasses of tea and Lutie singing to the sky.

"Chalk sounds so charming," said her mother. "And you're volunteering on Saturday. Who else is going?"

"I don't know much yet," said Doria. "How was work today? Anything interesting happen?"

Doria's mother thought everything was interesting, so she started right in. Updates on pesky colleagues, thoughts on intriguing romances, worry about maddening deadlines and vanished perks, photos of somebody's new baby.

The move here had not been anybody's first choice. Her dad, a research scientist at a pharmaceutical company, had been laid off. Her mother, a school librarian, had also been let go. Dad was crushed. He had thought he was vital to the team. He lost weight, began having chest pains and went back to smoking, twenty years after he'd quit. Her mother was so hurt that her posture changed, as if the school board had knifed her. Her shoulders got round and she gained weight and hated herself and hated her clothes and didn't want to see anybody.

They went through their savings in half a year.

And then her father was offered a job here. Doria hadn't wanted to move, but her parents said, "We're out of money, there's a job in Court Hill, get in the car." And before they even found a house, her mother walked into a library job at an elementary school only a half hour away.

Dad loved his new job because it was a job. Mom loved her new job because she loved books and kids and libraries, but also because nobody here had known her when she was slender. No one was wondering exactly how many pounds she'd put on.

Not only did Doria Bell live in a different world now, she lived with different parents. Her parents were careful, as if there might be snipers in the area, taking out jobs, and they had to keep their eyes peeled and their sleep light. No matter how valuable you were to your employers, you weren't that valuable.

Her parents wanted friends and allies. They were counting

on church, and church was coming through. They were so proud of Doria, getting that organ job at St. Bartholomew's. But they didn't want to drive all that way. They wanted to get to know their neighbors, and that meant First Methodist.

Can I do that too? she wondered. Give up the church job and the money and the applause and that great organ? Give up accompanying, the pleasure of it and the respect I get, and the responsibility? Can I get off the bench to join the crowd? Should I?

"Is there anything besides lemon chicken?" she said. "The sauce is too sweet for me. What else did you bring, Daddy?"

"Shrimp and scallops with ginger."

"Sold."

They cleaned up together, although with takeout, it was mainly filling the trash bag. Doria did a quick pass on the kitchen floor with the Swiffer, her mother started a load of laundry and her dad studied fridge and freezer contents, hoping for dessert.

Then Doria went to her room, to be alone with her laptop.

It took a minute or two of Googling, since she didn't know how to spell DeRade and she hadn't known there was an "e" on Greene. But the local newspaper site revealed all. DeRade Greene. Five-year sentence for wrapping a thirteen-year-old in barbed wire and blinding him in one eye.

Azure Lee believed that Train wanted to do that too?

Going off the track, she thought. It's possible. When I was standing on the sidewalk with him, first Train had a face and a laugh, and then he didn't. It's all in the timing, I guess. You don't want to be there when the tracks split.

She went back and forth between Nell and Stephanie's Facebook pages and got no closer to knowing what to say to them. If anything. What was a lost year compared to lost friendships?

Aunt Grace fixed dinner, which was unusual. She was an okay cook, but rarely in the mood for a stove. She knew every takeout in Ireland County. Tonight, she made corn bread with buttermilk. Spoon bread, rich and comforting, with plenty of butter.

The lost song plucked at Lutie. *Be you still alive?* it kept asking. She had a sense of MeeMaw crying out in the night. *Be you still alive?*

"You cut school?" said Aunt Grace mildly.

"Aunt Grace, did you make corn bread to soften me up?"

"Yes."

"I don't have an excuse."

Aunt Grace avoided Lutie's gaze, which was also unusual. Aunt Grace liked to nail people with her eyes. "How about an explanation, then?"

Aunt Tamika and Aunt Grace were terrified that Lutie would follow in Saravette's footsteps. Every time they looked at Lutie, they saw their failed, collapsed, sinful sister. The one with the most promise and the best looks. The one who'd found drugs instead, and then the gutter. Lutie couldn't stand their lectures. "I know better!" she'd snap.

"Saravette knew better too, and look what happened," they'd yell back.

Nobody knew who Lutie's daddy was, least of all Saravette. Saravette always wanted to try everything and everyone. Now she was just another homeless crackhead. Aunt Grace was always relieved when her sister was in jail. Jail is fine for some, she would say. Three squares and a cot.

It was Aunt Tamika who checked on their little sister every few weeks. She and Uncle Dean would cruise the neighborhoods where Saravette usually hung out. Drive by, tap the horn in a little pattern Saravette would recognize if she were conscious and felt like bothering. Aunt Tamika would provide Saravette with yet another prepaid cell phone. For a while, the sisters would chat away like girls in high school. Then Saravette would sell her phone or lose it and there would be a dark space when they heard nothing.

Lutie spooned up corn bread, trying to decide what to tell her aunt.

Even in Chalk, not that many people knew about Saravette. It was long ago and far away. People moved out and other people moved in. Babies were born and businesses were launched. Jail sentences were served and marriages began. Children went to college and into the army and moved to the city.

Even in Chalk, history was hard to see. The present was so noisy and demanding.

Sixteen years ago, MeeMaw had just suddenly been raising a baby. But so many grandmothers were, a person hardly noticed. The years went by and nobody cared who the mama was. Lutie had convinced herself that in her case, nobody even *knew* who the mama was.

But today a researcher had known. Lutie's birth to Saravette was on paper. Martin Durham had dug it up and it had led him to the music room at Court Hill High.

And there lay her skip-school excuse.

"Miss Veola wants to use the Laundry List to kick off her new church," said Lutie. "She wants publicity. She wants me to give a concert. I don't want to. I needed some time to think. So I went to MeeMaw's and sat on the steps." The truth, thought Lutie, but not the whole truth.

Aunt Grace, the most skeptical woman in the Carolinas, fell for it. "Lutie, what's wrong with giving a concert? I think it'd be great. I don't have a musical note in me. But I love to hear you sing. Everybody would love to hear you."

"Everybody says the Laundry List is a national treasure and I should turn it over. But it isn't a national treasure, Aunt Grace. It's my treasure."

"I don't own any?" asked Aunt Grace. "I'm a generation closer to Mabel Painter. Don't I get a vote?"

Lutie did not care for this. Aunt Grace and Aunt Tamika never sang the songs. No, they did not get a vote. "Mr. Gregg thinks it's time to record the songs," she said, moving right along. "To give Mabel Painter the place in American music history she deserves."

Aunt Grace was beaming. "Your MeeMaw would burst with pride! You could become a star."

Lutie wasn't so sure.

Mabel Painter's hymns were different. They weren't like the famous Negro spirituals so beloved by all races and countries—songs that spoke of black people immersed in the love of God. No questions, no rebellion. Just sweet heavenly acceptance. Songs like "Swing Low, Sweet Chariot" that said, It's okay, God. I can wait for death to have the good stuff.

Mabel wanted that sweet chariot too, and she knew that it would come and take her home. But hers were the songs of a woman starved for a decent life.

"Think of you being a star," said Aunt Grace. "I used to love the star song." In a scratchy metallic voice, halfway between pitches, Aunt Grace produced a strangled version.

"Big sky
Hard sky
Sky of small cold stars
You got a star for me, Lord?

109

I got scars instead, Lord.
I need my star, Lord!
Come shine for me, Lord!
Why you so far, Lord?"

And to Lutie's dismay, Aunt Grace wept.

I bet Saravette gave Aunt Grace those scars, thought Lutie. Aunt Grace knows when Saravette finished breaking all Ten Commandments. She knows who Saravette killed.

Is that why the Lord is too far away for Aunt Grace to go to church anymore?

Is Aunt Grace's sky just a lot of small cold stars?

Friday

Train plays *Slice the Tendons.*
Doria practices alone.

8

This time, when Doria obeyed Mr. Gregg's summons, he was standing with the short slim man who had been observing chorus the other day.

"This," said Mr. Gregg, "is my friend Professor Martin Durham."

The professor beamed at Doria and held out his hand.

Doria hated shaking hands, another of the many ways in which she did not feel normal. She nodded down at her book bag, her yellow plastic music carrier and her dangling purse, proving that she didn't have a free hand.

The professor kept smiling. "Your sight-reading at that chorus rehearsal was outstanding, Doria. And you accompany brilliantly. You always know exactly where your conductor is going and you're so well prepared. I'm envious of Mr. Gregg."

"Thank you," she said, trying to remember who had just warned her to be careful of charm.

"I'm told you are the organist at St. Bartholomew's," he went on. "That's an impressive position. I hope to hear you at the organ one day, Doria."

That was a fib. Nobody attended organ recitals, and even on Sunday mornings, nobody listened to the organist. During the prelude, the congregation talked or read the Sunday bulletin, hoping it would be a good hymn day and they would not be forced to sing junk. During the offertory, they hunted for their donor envelopes. During the postlude, they galloped out of the church.

"So, Doria," said Mr. Gregg, who detested pointless chatter, "did you ask Lutie about those songs in her family? That ancestral stuff?"

The truth is, thought Doria, Lutie must see to it that those songs survive, just as Mabel Painter saw to it that her family survived. It would be a privilege to help bring those songs to the world, but I have no business insisting on it. I'm white as a piece of paper. I'm supposed to tell Lutie what her black ancestor had in mind? "No," she said.

Mr. Gregg heaved a huge sigh. "We don't even really know what the songs are," he lamented. "Spirituals, I guess."

"Spirituals?" Doria frowned. "You mean, like 'Ah got a robe, you got a robe' or 'Soon Ah will be done with the troubles of the world'?"

"Mr. Gregg doesn't mean ancestors in the sense of all black slaves in the South," explained the professor. "He means specifically Lutie's great-great-grandmother, a woman named Mabel Painter. I'm trying to convince Lutie to record Mabel Painter's work for the music history museum I'm in charge of."

"You run a music history museum?" exclaimed Doria. "What a great job!"

"It is a great job. And it would be a great coup for me to get hold of those songs."

"Get hold." It was a very physical image: fingers gripping pages. There were no pages right now, but there could be.

And there could be recordings, too, because Doria herself could sing two of the Laundry List songs and hum a third.

She imagined singing to these men right now.

Her voice was slender and silver, like a child with a flute. Those songs needed Lutie, who could smite the notes like an Old Testament prophet.

But if Doria did sing for them? What then?

The professor would take the songs away.

Away to what?

Printing and publication. Recordings. Perhaps, but not necessarily, prestige. Perhaps, but not necessarily, money.

"It would honor Mabel Painter and her heritage," said the professor. "And we assume the works are religious, so it would also honor God."

No matter what the music teacher and the professor claimed, and no matter how much Doria liked these men, they didn't want the Laundry List for God, Mabel Painter, Lutie or America's musical heritage.

You want the songs for yourselves, she thought. So do I. What a trio we'd make: Mabel and Lutie and I.

In fact, why let Professor Durham or Mr. Gregg steal the songs, when Doria could steal them? If she wanted early admission to a fine music school, she could present those lost songs to the audition committee.

The idea jumped around in her head like an animated film, waving at her.

"Come on, Dore," said Mr. Gregg. "Lutie's your friend. Apply a little pressure."

Doria frowned. "What did Lutie say when you asked her for the songs?"

"She claims to know nothing."

The class bell rang.

Doria tried a Southernism. "Nice to meet you, sir," she said to the professor. "Y'all have a good day."

Professor Durham laughed. "It needs work, Doria. But I accept the thought."

Mr. Gregg followed Doria out of the music room. "Doria," he whispered, "Dr. Durham says that if I get him the folk songs, he'll introduce me to Broadway producers. My high school musical—the one I'm producing in the spring—*real producers will come hear it!*"

It's all about getting attention, thought Doria. That's what makes the world revolve.

I'm actually considering skipping my senior year in high school because I'm not getting enough attention. I even imagined stealing Lutie's songs in order to catch the attention of an audition judge.

She was so fond of Mr. Gregg. She did not want to contribute to this flaw in him, this need and greed. She wanted to pretend she did not share it. "Good luck," she said, not meeting his eyes. She scanned her phone, pretending she had exciting new messages, when in fact she was rereading old ones. Good thing, because she had entirely forgotten last night's message from the guidance office, reminding her that they wanted to see her today.

Doria normally avoided counselors the way she'd avoid a police chase. Keep a low profile and speed only on back roads.

She walked a few steps down the hall. Then she faded, and leaned against the wall for strength.

"Now what?" said Train.

She wasn't even surprised to see him. Mr. Gregg had called her out of class to meet the professor. It was a habit of his, since he did not believe that other teachers' subjects mattered. And here was somebody else who often cut class, being too busy frightening children, according to Pierce and Azure Lee.

Doria laughed. If only she could laugh like Lutie, gathering everybody up like a good meal. But she was stuck with the silent shaking of her shoulders. "I have to see the guidance counselor," she told Train.

He waved that away. "I already seen 'em today. They tired. They won't be any good to anybody now. Skip it."

This time Doria laughed out loud. She was not only attracted to Kelvin, who was in the grip of Lutie, but also to Train, who was in the grip of his slasher brother. She imagined sending *that* on to Nell and Stephanie. "Oh, Train, thanks for letting me laugh. You know, I'd rather use your real name. I'm told it's Cliff. I've never known a Cliff. Was it sort of a problem name? Is that why you dropped it?"

He said nothing.

They walked down the hall together. She glanced at him. His face had nothing on it and his eyes had nothing in them.

Although they had ordered Doria to be exactly on time, of course she had to wait. The waiting room had posters of colleges, leaflets with scholarship tips and a dedicated computer to search college websites and take virtual campus tours.

Following Pierce's suggestion, she picked a really big school. The University of Texas.

Doria did not know what her conference was supposed to be about. Schools loved conferences. It could be anything. Now she thought, I could ask about graduating in May.

Could she ask, when she had not even let her parents know it was on the table?

Was it on the table?

The story featured on UT's home page was "Geophysicists help Haiti prepare for the next big earthquake."

Yes! thought Doria. I'll be a geophysicist and help Haiti prepare for the next big earthquake!

"Doria Bell?" said a young woman. She was beautifully dressed. Very high heels. Excellent haircut. Probably sorry to be hidden away in a warren of tiny rooms and big files.

Doria, who tended to judge fast and harsh, did not think this woman would understand that Doria's life plan had just changed and that she needed to become a geophysicist right away.

The counselor sashayed into a tiny office. Her back was to Doria as she said, "How are you today?" Not the tone quality of a person who cared how Doria was today.

The woman did not introduce herself, but sat behind her desk and gestured Doria into a chair. Her name had probably been on the messages, and Doria should probably have read that far. Oh, well.

The woman looked serious. She pursed her lips in a tight little smile and handed over a list of Doria's outside activities.

How had she gotten all that information? And how was it the school's business what Doria did on weekends?

"Doria," said the counselor, "we're worried that you're over-scheduled."

What was the "over" part?

Doria was never late for her obligations. She never did poorly. She was outstanding in class. She was holding down a job as church organist and was a far better accompanist for concert choir than the adult Mr. Gregg had previously paid.

"It's a lot," said the counselor, tapping the paper as if it showed a series of flaws and failures.

A Southern girl would fill time by saying "Yes, ma'am," whether she agreed with the counselor or not. But Doria hadn't pulled off a Southernism with the professor, and the whole "ma'am" thing sounded like housemaids. So Doria stayed silent. She knew what the counselor was thinking now: Rude little Yankee. Why did they all have to move down here anyway?

The counselor frowned. "Do you think you're too busy?"

Doria frowned back.

"Just think about it," said the counselor, nodding in a satisfied way.

Doria stood up. She had not said a word. Had the woman noticed? Would she jot on Doria's folder: "Subject lacks verbal skills."

Doria left the office and headed slowly to her last class. The bell rang, and in a moment the halls were flooded with kids, and she was buffeted by their speed and sound. Suddenly she knew why kids quit school. They just got too tired one day.

"Hey, Doria," said Lutie, as they reached the chemistry classroom.

Doria found a smile.

"You're upset," said Lutie sharply, as if she had made other plans for Doria's day.

Doria chose to reveal the least of her problems. "The guidance counselor says I'm overscheduled."

Lutie giggled. "They never call in kids to say, 'You're underscheduled. You do nothing. You're a loser.' No, they call in the achievers. 'You do too much. We're worried! You might succeed!'"

Lutie told everybody in chemistry about Doria's encounter with the counselor. Everyone thought it was a hoot. Doria basked in the attention. Keep it up, she thought. Don't stop now.

But of course the teacher wanted to teach, and that was the end of Doria being the center of anything.

A few minutes before the final bell, the office called. "Doria, it's for you," said the teacher. "They want you to hurry. Nothing's wrong. Some church needs a substitute organist."

The class roared. "A church organ emergency?"

"It's probably a funeral," Doria explained, embarrassed. "Funerals can't be scheduled. Probably they couldn't find an organist. Probably they're desperate."

"It's a little thoughtless not to plan your funeral in advance," said one of the boys.

"But good to know that Doria can come to the rescue."

"Doria! Church organ hero!" Everyone laughed.

Doria was laughing too, and did not explain—because it was impossible—that she was already looking forward to playing an unfamiliar instrument. An organist cannot carry her instrument with her like a trumpet player. She has to work with whatever is in the church. No two organs are alike. Each sanctuary is different. Does it echo? Is it dead? Will the congregation belt out the hymns or just stand there?

The principal met her in the foyer. Sure enough, it was a funeral. "The minister will pick you up out front," he said. "I'll walk you out. I know him; I'm not sending you off with a stranger."

The final bell rang. A thousand kids poured out, paying no attention to anything in their path. Doria and the principal barely made it outside.

"Over here!" The man waving wore a clerical collar, unusual in this part of the world. Pale red hair, freckles, looked twelve years old. "Dane Haverford," the minister introduced himself. "You come highly recommended, Miss Doria."

"What happened to the regular organist?" she asked, expecting to hear that the regular organist couldn't leave work or had the flu.

"A horrible accident!" cried the minister.

Kids turned, wondering if they knew the person who had been in a horrible accident, and just how horrible it had been.

"The poor man was opening a tin can," said Dean Haverford, "and the lid slipped and he sliced his palm right down to the bone. He's at the hospital right now with surgeons trying to reattach the tendons."

Everybody flinched. Except one. Train mimed a slice through his own palm, let his hand and wrist dangle uselessly, and then laughed.

Lutie Painter was horrified.

Train had been handed a new idea. One quick slice and he could cripple somebody. An organist, a football player, a chef—well, anybody, when you thought about it—needed both hands.

Train grabbed the hand of some poor kid standing near him, and played Slice the Tendons. The kid tried to laugh. Train's friends did laugh.

Train might do it, too. Think what he had done to poor Nate. Well, sure, he claimed that he'd only cut the wire and that DeRade had cut the boy, but did anybody believe that? DeRade had had his brother in tow. Train would have been only steps away. And Train certainly had done nothing to prevent it, or he'd have barbed wire scars too.

DeRade had given himself a big gaping wound in his right palm. He'd been proud of it. Showed it to people. Didn't want a doctor. Didn't want stitches. Left the wound open.

What with the hole in his own fence and the hole in his own hand and the threats he'd made toward Nate to start with, the police didn't have to work all that hard to find the perpetrator. First thing they did was take DeRade to the ER for a tetanus shot, and after he started bragging about how Nate had learned a lesson now, DeRade was history. He went to prison grinning.

Doria Bell got into the car with the little-boy minister and drove away.

Train turned and caught Lutie's expression of contempt before she could wipe it off.

But maybe that's a good thing, thought Lutie.

He needed to know that he was despised.

The organ in Dane Haverford's church was in a pit, so the organist could see what was happening out in the church only by looking in mirrors. Doria edged down three tiny steps and maneuvered herself onto the organ bench. She opened her Mendelssohn.

Nobody would actually listen. People had important things to think about, like the dead person, and his life. Their own future deaths, and their lives.

What they wanted from Doria was filler. Something soothing and harmonious.

Bach could be grim and dark and intellectual. With Bach, you had to choose carefully. But Mendelssohn was always just right.

"We expect several hundred people," said Reverend Haverford.

How wonderful. Doria loved an audience.

She checked the rows of organ stops, chose an eight-foot flute and a four-foot flute for her right hand, a krummhorn for her left, what she hoped was a soft pedal stop (although she wouldn't know until she heard it), and a sixteen-foot diapason, and began playing the Mendelssohn G-major prelude, with its comforting lilt.

122

"Perfect," whispered Dane Haverford.

But it was not Mendelssohn she found herself playing. Chords formed, soft and round, rolling and repeating. *Mama, you sleep.* She moved from one key to another, changing manuals and stops. She segued into "Ain't Got No Sword," making it sad and slow, and wrapped up with "Take Me Home, Lord."

Afterward, the family came up to thank her for the beautiful music. What were the hymns? they asked.

"Um. Mendelssohn arrangements," said Doria.

When the funeral was over and Doria and Reverend Haverford left the church, the air had changed. The day was almost chilly. It smelled and tasted of fall. There was no hint of summer left in the brisk wind.

She had him drop her off in town. At the bank she cashed her check and smiled at the crisp bills. Who didn't love money? You felt as if you could go anywhere, do anything.

The weather said that Thanksgiving was coming, and frost, and that the time for jackets was here. Doria felt energized. She even felt athletic, as if she could have tried out for any varsity team and done well. But enough of all that fresh air. She let herself into First Methodist to practice.

Fridays were not a busy day at the church. Meetings were not held. Classes were not taught. The secretary and the minister had gone home.

She practiced a huge Bach prelude in C. It opened with a short pedal solo that required a leap of two octaves. She didn't look down at her feet, but got the right notes by memorizing the distance her knee and foot had to travel, putting the toe of her shiny organ shoe against the adjacent black note, and then pressing down on the correct white note.

She would never play this at St. Bartholomew's. They liked short little flutey things and quick sprightly trumpet things.

It was the most difficult piece Mr. Bates had given her. She worked and worked, while outside it grew dark and inside it was darker.

Her cell phone rang but she couldn't hear it. She had set it on top of the organ and saw the blinking red light. "Hi, Mom," she answered.

"Doria, honey, where are you?"

"Practicing."

"Doria! It's seven-thirty!"

"Oh. Sorry. Do you want to come get me?"

"I'll be there in a minute," said her mother, although it would take her ten.

Doria turned off the organ and rolled down the wooden lid. She slid off the bench, unlaced the black ribbons of her patent leather organ shoes, dropped them into their velvet shoe bag, slid her music into the ugly yellow plastic case and left the sanctuary.

Outside, it was very dark. The black asphalt of the parking lot reflected no light. The nearest streetlamp was far off.

The air was so crisp Doria felt as if she could see through the universe. She remembered what Mr. Amberson had said to Lutie's class, about stars and harmony. She stared up at the first handful of winking stars and thought of Mabel Painter, child of God.

Out on Hill Street, a car slammed on its brakes. Then it honked and turned hard into the church lot. It didn't slow down. Doria was caught in the headlights, frozen as a deer.

Her mother would never drive like that. She couldn't have gotten here that fast either. Doria made a fist around her key chain, so that an inch of shiny metal stuck out from between her knuckles.

The car braked hard and lurched to a stop. The window

came down. "Doria Bell," yelled Mr. Gregg. "What are you doing here, alone at night?"

"You scared me!" she shouted.

"Good. You ought to be scared, hanging out here by yourself. I thought you had half a brain, even though teenagers as a rule have only ten percent of a brain."

"I thought you liked teenagers."

"I do. That's why I work with them. Step one, I try to keep them alive."

"I'm perfectly fine," said Doria irritably. "Anyway, this is a nice town."

"With the usual allotment of scum. Get in. I'm giving you a ride home."

"My mother's on the way."

"Fine. I'll stay until she gets here and then I'll let her know that her daughter is standing around in an unlit parking lot in a lousy part of town."

"No! Don't say that to her. Anyway, it isn't a lousy part of town."

"Doria, you think crime and violence are jokes? You think a half inch of house key is going to stop a rapist or a mugger? Of course I'm going to tell your mother!"

Doria hated being corrected. "It was just you," she said sullenly.

"Doria, you know the boys in my Music Appreciation class? The ones taking it just to give me a hard time? You know anything about them? Train, for example. Formerly known as Cliff Greene. His older brother murdered somebody and got away with it, because there wasn't enough evidence to bring him to trial, even though DeRade boasted all over town. But DeRade's in prison after all because he blinded some little middle-school kid. Who knows why? Who cares why? DeRade likes to hurt people. And who do you think Train wants to be just like? You think Train looks at *you* and says, I wanna be like her—straight As, straight arrow. Guess what, Doria. Train wants to be just like his big brother, only worse."

"Okay, fine," she said. "I get the point."

"No, you don't get the point. It's a Friday night. Train and his kind are out in the dark, prowling, like any other kind of predator. He lives in Chalk, and Chalk is just down Tenth."

"There are fine people in Chalk," said Doria.

"That doesn't make it safe for you to be alone at night out here."

She was sick of all these people who didn't want her to practice alone.

Her mother turned into the parking lot. Mrs. Bell's headlights illuminated Doria chatting with somebody in a car. "Hi, honey!" she called. "Let's go! Daddy's worried. He doesn't like you practicing alone after dark."

"See?" said Mr. Gregg. But he didn't get out of his car after all, and he didn't talk to Doria's mother. Doria didn't have to lie about not doing it again.

Saturday
Morning and Afternoon
CHALK

Train gets in their face.

Saravette calls.

Lutie lets it go.

Doria walks worthy.

Kelvin half notices.

9

The taste of autumn was gone by morning. Saturday was hot, but not summer hot, when the air seemed to pull the marrow out of your bones and all your energy leaked away.

Lutie stood at the top of the hill in the shade of thick green magnolia leaves. The tiny chain-linked yards and grimy houses of Chalk spread out below. On a red clay lane, its surface as hard as pottery, sat Miss Kendra's dented old Ford Explorer. The big rear window was open and on the high shelf of the back were big metal casserole pans filled with chicken and rice, and a huge vat of green beans. A white plastic clothes basket packed with loaves of cheap white bread sat beside a cardboard box overflowing with homemade saucer-sized iced cookies.

The first time Miss Kendra served food in Chalk, people figured she was an undercover cop or else crazy. What kind of normal white woman drove right into Chalk, rolled down her car window, and yelled to the men sitting on their front porch playing cards and drinking beer, "Hey, y'all! Good evenin'! Got a hot dinner here. Want a plate? Chicken and biscuits."

"Yeah?" "Why?" "Who you?" were the usual responses.

It was kids who first began eating the meals, and only because they wanted the cookies. Miss Kendra would say, "Your mama want some dinner too? You want to take her a plate?"

They always wanted to take their mama a plate.

One Saturday Miss Veola came out to meet this intruder, and when the women ended up praising the Lord together, people relaxed.

Sometimes being relaxed in Chalk was a bad idea.

This neighborhood had crack houses, houses with crime tape across the front door, houses abandoned to rats, houses where anybody could be doing anything. And yet mostly it had houses full of sweet kids, a mama trying hard, and a baby-daddy stopping by now and then. It was a bad neighborhood but also a good one. People knew each other, and liked each other. They knew who to be scared of, and when. They knew who to check on, and when.

In Chalk, you always wanted company. And you always wanted fresh air, so the lawn chairs were gathered up close. Kids flowed from house to house and yard to yard like kids in the halls at school.

But Chalk could change in an instant. A gang moving down the lane wanted action. The sure way to get action was violence, or taunting that led to violence.

Gangs didn't care about a nine-year-old babysitting his little sisters. They didn't care about a ten-year-old practicing free throws to a netless hoop. They didn't care about an old lady on her front stoop, reading the obituaries. When you wanted action, you needed bystanders. If nobody saw it happening, it wasn't half as fun.

Chalk knew how to duck, but knowing didn't always save you. You could misjudge how long to lie low.

Today Chalk looked meager and tired. It had no vibe. It was just there, poor and crowded. Most strangers coming into Chalk today would want to dig in and change everything. But Miss Kendra wasn't trying to rework anybody's future or remodel anybody's choices. She had just been listening to the Lord one day, when he'd told her to take Matthew 25:35 seriously. "I was hungry, and you brought me food," Jesus had said. "Every time you feed a stranger, you are feeding me." And to Miss Kendra, he had added, "Start now. In Chalk."

In a minute, Miss Kendra would finish serving. The volunteers would get back in the Explorer and Miss Kendra would drive around the corner. It was safer on the next block. Mainly grandmothers. Although a fine grandmother could have a grandchild gone bad.

Lutie stood on the hill, thinking of grandchildren gone bad.

Doria Bell was having a wonderful time. She felt useful and good.

The speech of Chalk streamed around her like a slow-moving river. She felt like a turtle sunning itself on a flat rock, sweet water flowing by. She wanted to compose Chalk music, the music of voices in the dusty grass.

She separated a paper plate from the stack balanced on the edge of the open rear of the car. She took a big scoop out of the fifty-serving pan of rice. With a slotted spoon she scooped green beans from the hot water in which they sat. She arranged a big pink-iced cookie where it would not get damp from the beans and handed the plate to a towering black man with a gold tooth and swirling tattoos.

His face fell.

"More rice?" said Doria.

"No," he said, embarrassed. "No, ma'am, this is fine. Thank you."

"What? Tell me," said Doria. "This is my first time serving."

"I kinda wanted the yellow icing."

They both laughed. She traded the pink cookie for a yellow one.

A giggling kid whispered, "That pink one is a used cookie now, Miss Doria. Can I have it?"

She was so pleased to be called by name. She studied the little boy, realizing he was one of the kids who had been playing in Miss Veola's yard the other day. "You aren't the four-year-old," she said.

"I'm six. I'm Jayson."

"Jayson, I'm having a special on used cookies." Doria handed over the pink cookie. "But why are we whispering?"

"Miss Kendra doesn't let anybody have a cookie that didn't have their vegetable."

Jayson's brothers popped up. They wanted hot dogs and applesauce and were disappointed to find that Doria didn't have any. They looked suspiciously into the rice and didn't like the look of the herbs and sausage bits. And could that squishy thing be a mushroom? "We'll just have cookies," they said.

"Boys!" shouted Miss Kendra. "You march around here and let me see you eat those good vegetables first."

Doria gave them each a teaspoon of beans alongside a tablespoon of rice.

The boys ran around the Explorer to eat a bean or two in front of Miss Kendra. "Don't run out of cookies!" they hollered at Doria.

"I won't!" she hollered back.

Doria drank in the scent of sweet shrubs nearby, blossom-

132

ing like prom corsages. She served three more plates. Wiped her hands on a towel. Wiped her sweaty forehead with the sleeve of her T-shirt. And was badly startled by bright hard popping gunshot.

"Quander's family," said Miss Kendra. "They line up jars on the fence and shoot 'em."

Doria was shocked. "Isn't that dangerous? The houses are so close together! Is it even legal?"

"I don't think Quander's family cares whether things are legal. And it's only dangerous if you stand between the jars and Quander," said Miss Kendra.

Train waited for Doria to notice him.

First Doria had been distracted by the Waitlee boys and the cookie rules. Now she was standing with her shoulders tucked in, as if that would prevent Quander from thinking she was a jar.

Last month, Quander and Jerdoah Williams had been arrested on gun-related charges, but were out almost immediately on bail. Quander and Jerdoah thought the bail amount was a riot. They earned that much in a minute, selling drugs.

Now Miss Kendra was praying with a mama whose son was in the army.

The army was the best ticket out of Chalk, but you could get sent to a war zone. On the other hand, a son was in danger here in Chalk too, and didn't get paid like he would in the army. Miss Kendra was asking the Lord to watch over Wayne, and she and Wayne's mama were holding hands and swaying. When Miss Kendra prayed, people often sneaked a look at the clouds, because Miss Kendra was some pray-er.

Miss Kendra had been serving hot dinners in Chalk for a couple of years now, for no reason other than she felt like it.

Back when she'd started, everybody figured she was part of a sting. It was too strange—this white woman driving around Chalk yelling, "Hey, y'all! Want some dinner?" DeRade had never taken a plate. DeRade would rather starve than let somebody think he needed something.

"Why, hello, Train!" said Doria, beaming at him. "How are you? It's so nice to see you again." She fixed him a plate and held it out.

The terrible rage that could sweep through Train for any reason or no reason charred his heart. Just the sight of her white fingers on her white plate, her white smile as she took an hour out of her white life to help poor pitiful Chalk set him on fire.

He hated all volunteers at that moment, and all do-gooders, and anybody who prayed. He hated DeRade for blinding Nate and he hated Nate for ratting on DeRade. He hated Chalk and school and his mama and God.

After the barbed wire incident, Train's mama had stopped cooking. She had stopped being home, actually. Got a second job, worked all the time, kept the refrigerator and the cabinets full of food, but didn't fix it. "I went to church," she would say to him. "I took you. You and DeRade." She wouldn't cry. She'd just back away.

He was basically alone in the house with a lot of cereal boxes.

"That child blind!" Train's mama would shout at him if they crossed paths.

"I didn't do it!"

"You didn't stop it!"

It was not true that your mother would love you no matter what. His mother had stopped loving Train. She, like his teachers at school, was waiting for him to go away.

Doria served more plates. A woman hugged her. "God bless you," she said.

God had definitely blessed Doria.

But Train—no. God never thought of him.

He considered hurling the plate of hot food at Doria or Miss Kendra or the Ford Explorer and watching it spatter. It was a satisfying vision, and somehow enough. A little of the rage seeped away. Train took a bite of rice. It had a soft, spicy flavor and there was a bit of sausage along with the chicken and onions.

He saw that, around her waist, Doria wore one of those little hiker purses, a sort of zip pocket on a belt. The purse part had worked its way around her back. It was not all the way closed. The brass treble clef that held her keys was visible.

There was another volley from Quander's house. Doria whirled toward the sound, banging her arm and the serving spoon against the car. Train lurched into her, spilling the contents of his plate on her arm and the back of the Explorer. He reached out to steady her and instead got hold of the slotted spoon, flicking bean water over them both.

"Sorry," he said, taking her towel to mop up.

Miss Kendra was back from praying. Her eyes were narrow with suspicion, but she was not sure what to be suspicious of.

The inner burn that was stealing his flesh caught fire again. *Remember,* DeRade had said, *you're not going away. They can't get rid of you. You're in their face. You'll always be in their face.*

Train stood in Miss Kendra's face.

"Hop in the car, Doria," said Miss Kendra. "We're ready to drive to the next block."

Miss Kendra paused in front of a house that looked worse than any on the street. Debris poured out of it as if it were a garbage can, not a home. Two men sat on the porch, trash around their ankles. They were in shadow. Doria could barely make them out.

Doria wondered where Quander's yard was, and whether Miss Kendra was driving out of range, or into it. She thought of all the kids who'd decided against volunteering in Chalk. She thought of things she would not tell her parents about volunteering in Chalk.

"Good evening!" called Miss Kendra in the direction of the dark porch. "I got a fine hot dinner here. Y'all want a plate?"

The men cursed her.

Doria flinched.

Miss Kendra said softly, "They always say that, but I pray every week that their hearts will soften. The angrier you are, the sadder you are. I hate to see anybody that sad." She yelled out the window, "I baked the cookies myself. I iced 'em!"

The men said nothing.

Miss Kendra drove on. "Lord," she said, as if he were in the passenger seat, "guide their steps in your word. They want to walk worthy, they just don't know how to start. You help 'em out a little. If they can come get a plate, and know they have friends and neighbors, that would be a start. Wash their hearts, Lord. In Jesus' name. Amen."

Doria let the prayer repeat in her mind. She was beginning to see what Miss Kendra was up to. She was saying, I'm your neighbor. I'm glad to see you. Let's have dinner.

Doria had not tried to show kids at Court Hill High that they were worth her time and she was glad to see them. She had been waiting for *them* to do it. She was the new person, right? It was *their* responsibility.

She watched Miss Kendra.

No, she thought. It's always your own responsibility.

⌒

Train had never picked a pocket before. Or in this case, a purse.

He felt the weight of Doria's key chain in the deep pocket

136

of his sagging pants. Doria hadn't noticed a thing. And Miss Kendra, narrowing those old eyes and believing she knew something. Well, she didn't know anything.

It usually took Miss Kendra about two hours to work her way through Chalk, what with serving, chatting, praying, packing up and parking on the next street to do it all over again. Train figured he had an hour.

He changed his clothes fast. His mama hadn't bought him Sunday best for quite a while, but he'd gotten so thin, he could wear the old ones. A minute later he had crossed Tenth and was strolling through the CVS parking lot where Miss Kendra's volunteers would have left their cars. A person like Doria would be careful not to take up a slot meant for shoppers, so her car would be one of the three parked off to the side. And sure enough, there sat a Honda Accord, silver-gray, like half the cars in the lot. There on the front seat was Doria's ugly yellow plastic case. Train unlocked the car, got in and drove out Hill Street. With his right hand, he opened the plastic case. It was filled with music. Louis Vierne, said the top one. Symphony No. 1 for organ.

Train decided there was not a big secondary market for organ symphonies. He closed the case.

Five minutes later, he was at Home Depot. He checked himself in the rearview mirror. Clothing was fine. Hair, not so much. Nothing he could do about that now. Speech was the ticket now. You talked like them, they figured you were like them.

Train waited for the poky automatic doors to let him in and he walked down the wide front aisle, past lamps and tiles, appliances and plumbing, shelving and ladders, all the time separating the keys on Doria's key chain. He left the car keys on the ring. They weren't going to copy car keys for him.

He stepped up to a high desk where a pleasant-looking man in a cotton shirt didn't quite smile, wasn't quite sure.

Train smiled broadly. It actually felt kind of good, stretching his face sideways and letting the anger lapse. "Afternoon, sir. May I please have a copy of each of these?" He handed over what he assumed were church keys and a house key.

Now the man felt comfortable. "Weather still nice out there? I felt a bit of fall in the air when I drove in this morning."

"It's beautiful out," said Train, who never gave weather a thought and could not remember when he had last used the word "beautiful." "My mama thinks we might get a freeze," he added.

The man measured the keys against blanks, looking for matches. "My word. A freeze this time of year. I'm against it."

Train chuckled.

When the man was finished, he handed Train the copies.

"Thank you, sir. Y'all have a good day," said Train, smiling a second time, which was some kind of record.

Two male employees flanked the exit doors beyond the checkout lines. Train had not planned to pay but thought better of it. Receipt in hand, he walked sedately out of the store. Then he replaced Doria's keys on her key chain, started her car, drove back to the CVS, locked the Honda, trotted back to his house, yanked off his Sunday clothes, put his regular stuff on and jogged across Chalk toward Miss Veola's.

Miss Veola had an interesting set of visitors.

Train took another detour, avoiding them.

⌒

Lutie joined the little kids crowding around the back of the big red Explorer. "Hey, Doria," she said.

"Why, Lutie! It's so nice to see you!" Doria beamed at her.

"I'll have a plate, please," said Lutie. Lutie could lay claim to a bedroom at Miss Veola's, which was in Chalk, and she owned MeeMaw's house, which was sort of in Chalk, just across the creek. But since she really lived with Aunt Tamika and Uncle Dean, in a handsome development of massive brick houses on tiny lots with three-car garages and a clubhouse with a pool, Lutie taking a free meal from a do-gooder was just the kind of thing that made donors grumpy.

But Miss Kendra didn't care who ate what. It was like she was having a dinner party on the road and wanted company. "Lutie?" said Miss Kendra. Her deep accent turned it into *Loooo*-dih. "How you doin' in school, Miss Lutie?"

"Yes, ma'am, school's fine."

"Detail!" demanded Miss Kendra. "You applied for that magnet school, I know you did. You get in? You still studying science? I never took those classes, I don't even know how I graduated high school. I couldn't do it now."

"I didn't go after all," said Lutie, meaning the magnet school.

"What? Lutie Painter, I will have to follow this up. Why didn't you go?"

Lutie just laughed.

"Lutie here is a science scholar," Miss Kendra told Doria.

"Guess what," said Lutie. "Doria's ten times the scholar I am."

"My word! Doria! And you took time off study to help me serve? The Lord bless you and keep you."

Lutie's smile tightened. She had a bad feeling about this afternoon. And she didn't trust the Lord to bless and keep Doria.

Train made it with time to spare.

Miss Kendra had reached the farthest block, and was now visiting Miss Elminah, who lived alone. She'd painted her windows shut for safety, making her place so musty she spent all her waking hours outside, calling "Hey" and hoping for visits.

It was getting dark.

In the dark, on a Saturday, when the men had been drinking and losing at cards and doing drugs, it was stupid for Miss Kendra to be here. Train figured she had lost track of how early it got dark these days.

Miss Kendra said, "Why, hello, Train. You come for seconds?"

"No, thanks," said Train, who hadn't said thank you in two or three years. He raised Doria's key chain. "Found this in the road. Anybody here lose it?"

"Why, those are mine!" cried Doria. "Oh, my goodness. I didn't think I was that careless. Thank you so much, Train! I'm so grateful!"

He set them neatly in her outstretched hand.

"We got one more street to visit," called Miss Kendra briskly. "We got to see Miss Veola before it's full dark. My team, get in the car now. Train, you flirt with Doria Monday in school."

Train was horrified that anybody could think he was flirting with Doria. He almost fell over his feet backing up.

"We got to get to Peter Creek," said Miss Kendra, bundling Doria into the backseat of the Explorer.

Half the roads around here were named for the creeks that ran through narrow gullies. The streams were shallow or dried out in midsummer, but there had been lots of rain this year, and they ran fast and full. It was Peter Creek that divided old Miz Painter's house from Chalk. Miss Veola's little pink church sat on a tiny gurgly branch of Peter Creek, which liked to flood and tear soil from tree roots and then settle back to a trickle.

"Who is Peter Creek?" asked Doria, getting in the car.

What a loser, thought Train.

⟋

Lutie frowned.

Since when had Train become a Boy Scout, helping old ladies cross the street and returning lost keys to ditzy girls?

Train put on his sunglasses. They were large and opaque. Half his face was hidden now, which was probably the point. "You maybe want to visit Miss Veola too, Lutie," Train said. "She got a visitor come just for you."

Lutie's heart stopped. Saravette is here, she thought.

She put her own sunglasses on quick, and she and Train stood facing each other. They couldn't see each other's eyes.

He knows, thought Lutie. I can't stand it that anybody knows! But why does Train have to be the one who knows? I wouldn't trust him with a shoelace, never mind my life.

She walked away fast. She had to get to Miss Veola's and do whatever damage control she could.

She was halfway there when she remembered that Train had held Doria Bell's key chain before. He would have recognized that brass treble clef. He would have known it was Doria's. He wouldn't have had to ask who had lost it.

Miss Kendra had been right. Train had been trying to flirt with Doria.

Miss Veola was surrounded by a court of elderly ladies, plump, well-dressed and fussy. Behind them, the sun was setting. Gaudy pinks and purples with threads of gold exploded behind tinted clouds.

Doria ran into Miss Veola's yard as if they were old friends.

"Good evening, Miss Doria," said a voice from the shadows.

"Professor Durham?" she said incredulously.

There was that great smile, twinkly and carrying. "I'm working on my project, Doria. In my travels I heard about Reverend Mixton, and how she's turning a movie theater into a church, and I had to stop."

Doria had not known Miss Veola's last name. An oddity of the South was that you might never learn last names.

"Hey, Dore," said another voice.

"Mr. Gregg, you're here too?"

"Miss Veola and I are buddies. She's had at least one and sometimes a dozen kids from her church in my music program every year and she's never missed a concert."

"Which one is your church, Miss Veola?" asked Doria. You couldn't turn a corner here without finding another church. They had the most romantic names. Liberty Freewill Baptist. Red Bluff AME Zion. Mount Tabor Holiness.

"It's down the road a piece. People call it the pink church. I was just a slip of a girl when I founded it. My dear friend Eunice gave me the courage to do it. Eunice was Lutie's MeeMaw."

"I haven't seen any pink church," said Doria.

"Pink on the inside," said Miss Veola. "Brick on the outside."

The professor and the elderly ladies went back to exchanging family histories. Surely they were distantly related, or had once had next-door neighbors who were related, or at least had had Sunday-school teachers who had taught an in-law. They had reached the stage when they were determined: somehow they would come up with a cousin in common.

Professor Durham made his move. "I'm filled with hope that I am getting close at last to the lost songs," he said.

The friendly ladies smiled and rocked and hummed. They sipped tea and stirred ice cubes.

They have to know, thought Doria. Last week they must have listened to Lutie sing, not to mention all the weeks and years before.

Miss Kendra, having served a half dozen plates, bustled into the yard. "I heard the news, Veola! I am so excited! Trees clap hands and sing!"

Doria was glad she'd had a lot of church exposure, so she knew a Bible quote when she heard one and didn't have to worry about Miss Kendra's sanity.

"What's the news?" asked Mr. Gregg.

"We got an offer on the pink church," Miss Veola told him. "Pastor Craig's congregation is buying it. Now they can move out of their storefront and we can move into our new church even earlier than I was thinking." Miss Veola nodded approvingly at the Lord.

"Praise the Lord!" cried Miss Kendra, and now all the ladies stood, praising God, all talking out loud at the same time. Doria loved the crossing voices and the jumbled words.

The professor did not pray but leaned back in his plastic chair, a researcher soaking up atmosphere.

When the prayers ended, Miss Kendra said, "How about plates tonight, ladies? I have such good food!"

"Honey, thank you, but I brought us a big pan of chicken to share," said one of the old ladies. "I can fry chicken, if I do say so. And corn bread! Who wants some of my corn bread?"

The professor introduced himself to Miss Kendra. "Miss Veola's been telling me about your hot meal ministry, and of course I think you're good-hearted, but I am surprised that your actions are legal."

Miss Kendra stiffened.

"In my part of the world," said the professor, implying

that his part of the world was better and more sophisticated, "when serving the public, you are required to cook in a kitchen inspected by the state, not in somebody's house where there could be any standard or no standard. You'd certainly have to have warming ovens in your van to keep the meals at a prescribed temperature. In fact, you'd have to be licensed."

I bet he's right, thought Doria.

Her heart sank. She thought of the happy children eating beans to get cookies. The man who had been so hungry he ate right off his paper plate, not even waiting for a plastic fork. The teenager who'd come back to get plates for his mama and sisters. The woman who had saved a piece of her own birthday cake to give Miss Kendra in return.

"By now," said the professor, "in this heat, I don't know but what that food hasn't gone bad."

"You plan to build a soup kitchen for us?" demanded Miss Kendra. "You plan to give me the money so we can serve our neighbors with the appliances you passed a law saying we have to have? I'll take your check right now, thank you."

⁀

Train followed Lutie toward Miss Veola's.

Since there was nothing Lutie liked more than visiting Miss Veola, and since she was Mr. Gregg's pet, Train had expected her to dance right up, sit right down.

Instead Lutie stopped short in the middle of the road, caught in long shadows.

A dude in a suit was yelling at Miss Kendra. A minute ago, Train had hated her for driving in here all white and show-offy: *You can't cook your own food, you losers. You need me.* But now he liked her, yelling back at the man in the suit instead of being all prayer-y and Jesus-y.

144

Who was the guy? An inspector?

Train despised authority. If the guy was here to shut Miss Kendra down, Train just might have to slash his tires. He might do it anyway. He hadn't done it in a while.

A silver Audi was parked by the corner. Definitely the suit guy's car. It cried out for vandalism.

"I'm so sorry," said the suit guy to Miss Kendra. "I did not mean to touch a nerve."

Come on, you totally meant it, thought Train.

Raw nerves grated like crickets in the grass. Doria did not want this beautiful afternoon ruined. She would wait in Miss Kendra's car. She eased back to the gate and put her hand on the latch. Down the tiny twisting lane, the sun slid away and children danced in the dust, watching their shadow selves cavort.

She thought of Miss Kendra's prayer. *They want to walk worthy.*

So she walked back. "Professor Durham? I am proud to be allowed to volunteer for Miss Kendra. I didn't do any work, I just put food on plates. But people smiled. I think dinner was just the right temperature. It was the temperature of —well— being neighborly."

〜

Rats. I have to be friends with her now, thought Lutie. Burden or not.

But she couldn't move. Couldn't join Doria and second the motion. Her relief that none of the visitors was Saravette made her flimsy.

If Miss Veola had produced the Laundry List for him, Professor Durham would not be discussing bacterial food poisoning. So the Laundry List still belonged to Lutie Painter.

In her pocket, her cell phone vibrated. She checked it. She and her girlfriends were in touch every few minutes.

But this was no girlfriend.

It was Saravette.

Stop it! thought Lutie. Don't call me! I don't want you. Not here or anywhere else.

⟲

Footsteps.

Hard-soled shoes, tapping evenly on the surface of the road.

Not a kid. Kids wore sneakers or Crocs or flip-flops.

A cop, thought Train.

He stayed motionless, well behind Lutie.

But it was only Kelvin, as big and noisy as any intruding adult. Well, he was intruding. Kelvin didn't live in Chalk. His daddy moved out before he was even born, and Kelvin was slumming here, just like Doria. Just like Lutie, for that matter.

"Hey, y'all," said Kelvin, his voice as fat and thick as his body. Probably still wanted to be a preacher and listen to his own voice all day.

"This is one of my baritones, Professor," said Mr. Gregg. "Kelvin."

Doria turned to greet Kelvin. The lowering sun gleamed on her pale face. Everything showed, as if Doria's skin had come off.

That girl adored Kelvin.

What was it about stupid Kelvin?

Doria's crush smothered her. But Kelvin hardly noticed her. "Well, hey there, Doria," he said. "And Mr. Gregg!" He offered the music teacher a handshake.

How large his hand was. Doria changed her mind about shaking hands. She wanted to stick her hand out for the pleasure of holding Kelvin's.

"Kelvin," said Mr. Gregg, "this is Professor Martin Durham. He's researching the Laundry List."

"My daddy used to love those songs. Miz Eunice, she'd set on her porch and sing. I can sort of remember but not really. Mostly I remember my daddy talking about it."

"Is your daddy a baritone too?" said the professor. "Can he sing the songs for me?"

Kelvin laughed. You could go swimming in a laugh as deep and warm as that. "Who would want my daddy to sing, when you've got Lutie? Lutie has the best voice in the whole wide world."

"Lutie's being contrary," said Mr. Gregg.

"Oh," said Kelvin. "I'm Lutie's shadow, so I guess I'll be contrary too."

Miss Veola raised her eyebrows. "Lutie's shadow?"

"When you're as good at things as Lutie," said Kelvin, "everybody is in your shadow." He smiled at Doria. "Unless you're casting a pretty big shadow of your own. Like Miss Doria."

Doria wanted to hurl herself into his arms, but instead she gestured toward Miss Kendra's car. "Do you want a plate, Kelvin?"

"No, thanks. I just went to Burger King. I'd take a cookie, but I know Miss Kendra's rules. And I'm not in a vegetable mood."

Doria decided to learn how to bake cookies. And ice them.

⌐

Lutie opened Miss Veola's little gate with unnecessary force and shut it loudly behind her. "Good evening," she said, like a trumpet. "Why, Professor Durham. And Mr. Gregg." She used her Chalk voice: *Whaaah, Professah Door-Ham. Ayund Mistah Grayyg.*

Doria and Kelvin regarded her thoughtfully.

"Miss Lutie," acknowledged the professor. "I was just about to ask Miss Doria about her own music."

"Sir?" said Doria, grasping at last the value of Southern styles of address. So courteous and yet so distant.

"Mr. Gregg showed me one of your compositions, Doria. A person of your scope belongs in the High School of Performing Arts. Your talents are wasted at Court Hill High."

I am lonely at Court Hill High, thought Doria. But I am not wasted. Musically I have moved a long way in a short time. And musically, Mistah Door-Ham, I am ahead of you. I own some of the Laundry List myself.

"Right now, on the organ," said Doria, amazed to hear a Southern drawl in her own voice, "I'm doin' some Buxtehude, a little Mendelssohn and of course Bach."

Kelvin butted in. "You know, Doria, you want real music, you should come to Miss Veola's church one Sunday. I'll take you. Lutie, she can shout down that aisle."

Kelvin would take her? Doria almost leaped on top of him so they could piggyback over to the church right now. "I can't. I have a church job of my own."

"Don't sound so sad about it," said Miss Veola. "You're doing the Lord's work."

"For you, it's probably the Lord's work. But I'm just showing up. I love to play the organ and I love an audience. I'm not sure I love God. In fact, I usually forget he's there, I'm so busy with the notes."

This was very distressing. The ladies climbed right on board. A soul was at risk. They dug deep.

148

Professor Durham and Mr. Gregg gave up and left.

Lutie said suspiciously, "Doria? You offer up a little god-lessness just to change the subject?"

Miss Veola said, "Shame on you, Doria Bell."

"Way to go, Dore," said Kelvin.

Kelvin enjoyed the scenery of the two girls. It tickled him that Lutie was associated with something called a laundry list. Lutie seemed more of a candidate for a Treasures of the Nile list or a Jaguar list. A Star in the Sky list. A How Many Guys Can Have a Crush on the Same Girl at One Time list.

In the long shadows of early evening, the two girls seemed to change colors. The white one went black and the black one went gold.

How beautiful the world is, thought Kelvin, utterly satisfied with life.

He turned to leave and saw Train, alone in the road, swaying like a cobra.

Saturday
Night

Train prowls.

Doria practices alone.

Lutie plays the message.

Aunt Tamika tells the truth.

10

The sun had set.

The guests were gone.

Lutie turned on her pastor. "You had no right to talk to that musicologist."

"Rights!" shouted Miss Veola. "You have rights to that music? What rights? You got a will, maybe? A last testament? A deathbed video?"

Miss Veola never yelled. Lutie was stunned. "No, ma'am. But it's my music, isn't it?"

Miss Veola lowered herself into a lawn chair. In the faint light of dusk, the pastor looked a hundred years old. "Lutie, Professor Durham is different. The other researchers were just wandering by. Your MeeMaw just stood there and looked ignorant until they were gone. This man will dig to China if that's what it takes. But it won't. He knows he's on the right track. He'll go from house to house. He'll offer money or TV interviews or just a bottle of liquor. One by one, he'll collect your songs. And then, Lutie, the Laundry List will be his."

Lutie did not want to hear this.

"He'll call them folk songs. Mabel Painter probably sang

them, he'll say, but anybody could have composed them. All the women in Chalk did laundry, he'll remind us. These pieces were probably composed jointly. Besides, he'll add, Mabel Painter lived in the nineteenth century. This is the twenty-first. The songs are public domain."

Lutie was filled with dread, as if she'd been walking through the woods and looked up to see a snake draped overhead.

"And then he'll point out that he's the only one who bothered to collect them. If the young Painter woman had cared about those precious songs, she would have done it herself."

"Did he say that?"

"It's the way of things. Music collectors have always scoured the countryside for folk music. Hungarian. Appalachian. When some old Eastern European peasant woman sang her lullaby or some old shepherd on a Scottish moor sang his ballad, you think the researcher took names? Wrote checks? No. He went home and presented the songs as folk music, meaning they belong to anybody and everybody. The copyright will go to the researcher. The way things are shaping up, Lutie, you're going to be informed that the Laundry List was given to the community of Chalk over the years and now Chalk is giving it back. Perhaps its new curator will make mention of Mabel Painter, or Eunice, or you, and perhaps not."

"That's theft!"

"You won't be able to prove theft," said Miss Veola, "because you never established ownership."

The word "ownership" was stiff and formal. Lutie hardly knew what to make of it.

Mabel Painter had owned so little.

Snatches of melody and words thrust themselves at Lutie. Some were notes she had forgotten. Some felt unsung, as if she possessed melodies she hadn't heard yet.

Lutie saw Mabel Painter standing in the meadow, telling God that she did not want more scars.

Give me my star! cried Mabel Painter.

Give me my star! cried Mr. Gregg.

Give me my star! cried Professor Durham.

We all want stars, thought Lutie. Except maybe Train. Train might actually want the scars instead, like the scar DeRade has in the palm of his hand, proof forever that he blinded Nate.

"How can the Laundry List make him a star?" she protested. "The songs don't have million-seller potential. They won't work on some huge stage with a backup band and pyro-technics. All they are is one woman's hymn to her God."

"So is every hymn and carol in the world. But the world sings 'Silent Night' a million times every Christmas," said Miss Veola. "Lutie, I know you're sick of me by now. But if you per-form the Laundry List, it would fill our church. It would bring our people together. It would help the lost find God. It would bring joy and yes, it would bring money. But most of all, it would establish you as the source of the songs." Miss Veola paused. Then she said softly, "You know what your grand-mother wanted. For you to use your wood for something good."

Miss Veola was referring to the saddest of the songs. The song where Mabel Painter admitted that a Negro laundry-woman wasn't a real person with real feelings and real hopes. She wasn't any different from a stick of kindling to heat the water. She was a laundry tool.

I am wood, gentle Jesus.
This world, they say I am wood.
Wood don't feel no pain. Wood don't weep.

Lord Jesus, the world, they say I am wood.
Wood don't have heart, wood don't have
    hope.
The world, they say I am wood.

If I am wood, gentle Jesus,
Use my wood.
Use my wood for something good.

Lutie was always shaken by the presence of Jesus in the song. If Jesus was so gentle and if he was also the Lord God Almighty, how come Mabel Painter was just a stick of wood? Why didn't he intervene?

Lutie could hardly see past all those notes. "There's a song I half know," she said slowly. "I can't quite pull it back. It started playing inside me a few days ago. Do you remember one that starts with the words 'Be you still alive'?"

Miss Veola took a long slow drink from her glass. By now, it must be all melted ice, and no tea. "I think we've probably lost a number of songs, Lutie. One I half remember is about six more days. It was a countdown song. The only day Mabel Painter could be off her feet was Sunday, the seventh day. So each day of the week was one fewer to wait for Sunday. But I don't know the words anymore, or the melody."

"What church did Mabel go to? The churches around here don't seem old enough."

"I don't think they had a building, only an arbor. Vines on a trellis. I feel as if somebody told me the vines were wisteria. Would have been violet and mauve. Probably had birds nesting. I think they'd have sat on something, because they were laborers. It really was their day of rest. But there wouldn't have been pews." Miss Veola struggled to her feet. "I'll give you a ride home, honey."

Miss Veola had kept her Cadillac washed and polished and running for a quarter of a century. When she came out of her house with her purse and had locked the door behind her, they climbed in. Miss Veola gave her leather upholstery a little pat.

Lutie had a sudden vivid memory of MeeMaw sitting here in the front seat, and the two old friends giggling like seventh graders. "Be you still alive?" she asked again. "I have a few notes of it." She hummed, but her memory did not locate the rest of the melody.

"You staying with Mika or Grace tonight?"

"It doesn't sound like a hymn," said Lutie. "And I feel as if you have to cry when you sing it. I think it's a weeping song."

"Which way am I driving, Miss Lutie?" said the pastor. "Tamika's or Grace's?"

"Aunt Tamika's."

They left Chalk. Miss Veola took a long slow turn and a long slow time.

"Maybe Aunt Tamika will remember 'Be You Still Alive?'," said Lutie.

A mile later, Miss Veola said, "I don't want you to bother your aunt. Yes, it was a weeping song. No, it isn't part of the Laundry List. Your MeeMaw songed that up."

"MeeMaw wrote songs too?" Lutie was amazed and excited.

"No. She sobbed on the porch for years after Saravette left for good. And one day, the pain found notes." Miss Veola turned into Aunt Tamika's driveway and let the car idle. "You were a baby. Saravette was doing drugs and selling them, selling herself too, doing everything bad there was to do, and she and her mama had a terrible fight. Saravette stormed away and never came back. Never called. Never wrote. Never sent a message. Knowing how Saravette chose to live, and what she was doing to her body and soul, your poor MeeMaw didn't even know if her baby girl was still alive. Eunice hid her sorrow

157

in her heart because it wouldn't be good for her baby Lutie to be raised in all that grief. But it came out in song."

In her youth, Miss Veola had been a singer, but youth was decades ago. She struggled for breath.

"Be you still alive, my sweet sweet girl?
Be you coming home?
My heart hurts more than broken bone.
More than crash and burn.
Be you still alive, my sweet sweet girl?
Be you coming home?"

MeeMaw. On the little porch, with its bright red flowers in their blue cans, and the meadow stretching out. Be you still alive? she had cried to the dark sky and the dark unknown. Be you coming home?

Lutie wept. "And did Saravette come home when MeeMaw was still alive? I don't ever remember her being around."

"Once."

"Was I there?"

"No."

"Were you there?"

"No."

Lutie touched the slender rectangle of her cell phone inside her pants pocket. She had not answered Saravette's phone call an hour ago, but Saravette had left a message. Why couldn't you have sent messages to your mama when she needed you? Lutie thought, hating Saravette. Why were you so mean?

"Run on in," said Miss Veola, and Lutie knew that the old woman needed to cry. Whether for Saravette or Eunice or the world, Lutie did not know.

Lutie let herself into the house. Saravette had come home

once? How cruel. But maybe it had been a good visit, and that was why Saravette had stayed in the area.

The garage door opened. Lutie was so glad not to be alone anymore. Aunt Tamika and Uncle Dean were back from a satisfying Saturday of shopping. "You have a good day?" said Aunt Tamika, kissing and hugging her and hanging up plastic dress bags.

"Yes, ma'am."

"Anything happen?" asked Uncle Dean.

"No, sir."

"I got a text this afternoon from Miss Veola," said Aunt Tamika. "A professor wants to record the Laundry List? Sounds to me like something happening."

Lutie felt the strong women in her life and history calling to her. Do something with your life! Sing! Study! Star! Get your ticket out!

How envious she was of girls who were not trying, who let life puddle around them while they laughed, and did their hair, and had boyfriends.

"Here's how I look at it," said her uncle. "You make a name for yourself with the songs. You use the recordings to get into a top-tier music conservatory." He set packages on the kitchen counter and admired the shopping bags. "On the other hand, I'm not sure I want you majoring in music. You have to think of jobs, Lutie, and a decent income. Expertise in science might be a better ticket. You can always do music on the side."

It's Saturday, thought Lutie, and the professor drove away from Chalk. He could maybe come back tomorrow afternoon and cruise around, song-hunting on a Sunday. But he has to be at work Monday through Friday. That gives me a week, anyway.

Her aunt harped on the Laundry List. "You know, Lutie,"

she said, "to whom the Lord has given much, from that girl much is expected."

"I'm giving a ton," snapped Lutie. "I'm getting terrific grades. I'm winning prizes. What more do you want? Anyway, Saint Paul was not referring to music."

"Wow," said her uncle. "Maybe nothing was happening today, but all that nothing sure got you stirred up."

"What do you want for dinner?" asked Aunt Tamika, trying to make peace.

"I ate. I had a plate from Miss Kendra."

"Now, there's a strange woman," said Uncle Dean.

Lutie wanted to tell them what the professor had said to Miss Kendra and what Doria had said back. But she had never mentioned Doria to her aunt and uncle, and Doria took a lot of explaining. Meanwhile, the cell phone in her pocket weighed so much with its silent hovering message from Saravette that Lutie thought maybe her pants seam would rip.

She flopped down on the sofa to text everybody and see what they were doing tonight.

Miss Kendra drove Doria back to the CVS where Doria's mother's Honda was parked. "You were the best volunteer, Doria. You worked hard, you were cheerful and you made friends with little kids. I'm going to use what you said in our newsletter. 'The temperature of being neighborly.'"

"I had a good time," said Doria. She had had a profound time, but you were not supposed to say things like that. Although maybe with Miss Kendra you could.

Miss Kendra waited in her car until she heard Doria's engine turn over, then honked her horn in farewell and drove away.

Doria drove out of the CVS parking lot. When she reached her driveway, she remembered that her parents had joined First Methodist's revolving dinner club. Tonight was their turn to bring the main dish, and her mother had labored over it as if the future depended on what she brought.

What *does* the future depend on? wondered Doria.

The day had been so full, so busy—yet it was only seven o'clock on a Saturday. Everybody else in the world was doing something interesting. Movies. Parties. Friends.

Friends like Nell and Stephanie. Failure to text was failure to care. They had shrugged about violin and shrugged about French horn and now they were shrugging about her.

The friends of this afternoon—if they had been friends—had evaporated like a puddle in the road. Now she had to sit alone in an empty house, where solitude would slap her in the face. Doria turned the car around and headed back to Court Hill to practice.

First Methodist was dark and silent.

Doria parked and got out of the car. The heat of the day had not dissipated, and the dark had a warm enveloping feel. She let herself into the church and locked the door behind her. Her footsteps were silent on the carpeted aisles.

A show-offy mood came over her. She didn't want to learn new notes; she wanted to hear herself shine. Prove she had something to offer.

She started with a Handel symphony, the one in F, in which sparkling flutes danced all over the keyboard. It had a brutal pedal part. Her toes and heels darted up and down the fat wooden pedal board. The corners of each page had been turned so many times that the final measures were discolored from her fingerprints.

Then she played a huge Bach prelude, also in F, which opened with a massive pedal solo. Doria had to grip the bench to keep her balance.

The church rocked.

Now the last movement of her Vierne symphony: music to bring down a ceiling, and an audience.

⌣

Train prowled.

Night had become more comfortable than day. By day, you were on display; your body and your face and your failures were right up front, where teachers and preachers and parents and the competition could stare at you, and judge you. By night you were shadow, safe inside your skin.

In Chalk, many preferred the night. People leaned on cars and slouched on porches, visiting. Everybody seemed slow. Slow to speak, slow to move, slow to think. Train took out his knife and played with it. His own hands seemed slow.

In a vacant lot, a fire had been lit in an old oil barrel. Men had gathered around, talking softly and laughing.

Train thought of the TV clip where that kid became his own bonfire. Where the parents of the boys who'd set him ablaze kept saying into the camera, "Our sons didn't do it!" But Train could tell. They knew their kids had done it.

Once, in elementary school, there had been a bonfire fundraiser. Train had had his first s'more. He loved toasting that marshmallow, pressing it down with a chunk of chocolate, careful not to snap his graham crackers. He remembered how he'd wolfed down the s'more as the bonfire wolfed dry wood.

He drifted, skirting the circles of light from streetlamps. On the move, like a predator, like a panther or jackal easing through the grass in the night.

And there, in the parking lot at First Methodist, was the Honda Train had stolen earlier that day. It was the only car in the lot.

He chose a door that he felt would not open directly into the sanctuary. When he put his hands on the door, it was vibrating. Doria must be making some serious noise.

Train put his shiny new key in the lock and it turned.

He was in a windowless hallway, which was lit by EXIT signs at each end. A long low table was covered with pamphlets, crayon bags, name tags and a basket of markers. There was a couch for people who had to leave in the middle of a service to calm a crying baby, or who needed to cry themselves.

To his left was a big wooden door with a small square glass window. Train peeked through the window and saw that he was at the rear of the sanctuary. Pews spread down two aisles. The organ was at the opposite end, high and exposed. There were lights both under and above the music rack and at the organist's feet. Everything else was dark.

Doria was a slim shifting silhouette, eyes fastened straight ahead on the music. He marveled that she could produce all those notes without glancing down. It didn't look as if she could even see her flying feet because the keyboard projected out over her lap.

He cracked the door. Music flooded out, as if he had breached a dam. Immense shuddering chords assaulted him. Train eased inside and held the door carefully, so that it closed soundlessly. Not that Doria could possibly hear a door. She must be drugged from all that sound. Train blinked, getting used to the layout, and out from behind his eyes came the dead eye, the eye of Nate.

Course, Nate still had the other eye. It was probably enough.

Train was no longer hot and burning. He was shivering,

like some little kid locked out of the house in the rain. He could not reverse what he and his brother had done. His only hope—although "hope" was a pretty word, and Train had nothing pretty in mind—was to do something worse. If it piled up high, wide and ugly, the aggregate of his crimes would be impressive.

He would be the baddest.

He would fill the whole category and people would respect him.

He would no longer wake up at night wondering what it had felt like when the barbed wire pierced Nate's eyeball.

His finger slid along the blade of his knife, but his inner vision turned again to fire, those boys tossing a little fuel on a T-shirt, and *whoompf!* A living torch running down the street.

If you were going to be the baddest, you might as well do something that would make a good video.

⟋

Aunt Tamika and Uncle Dean loved to cook. They discussed in detail whether they had the right ingredients and who would do what. Tonight they were grilling salmon. Uncle Dean went to the patio to turn on the grill. Aunt Tamika started chopping vegetables, and they called back and forth about a sauce decision.

They had one of those killer kitchens where you could really cook.

Killers, thought Lutie, feeling again the weight of her cell phone. The message she had not listened to stuck up like the tines of a pitchfork left in the grass.

Aunt Tamika and Uncle Dean were peeling and measuring and stirring.

164

Lutie lay on the sofa, and now at last she played Saravette's message.

"Lutie?" Saravette said it like Miss Kendra: *Loo*-dih? With that little question mark. "I've done bad things, baby girl. I'm trusting Miss Veola and Tamika and Grace to be sure you don't. Some of the bad things I meant to do, and some I've done a thousand times and I didn't care then and I don't care now and I had fun. But one of the bad things—I'm so sorry." Saravette's voice cracked. "It was an accident, Lutie. Or maybe not. I've never known. It happened and there I was. Lutie, honey, the other day, I couldn't talk to you after all. I meant to talk. But I was scared of you. Things ain't good for me, Lutie. But I want you to know that I want things good for you."

The voice tapered away, as if Saravette were leaving the phone and the room. Or hoping Lutie would pick up.

"Been remembering the list," said Saravette. "Mama singing on the porch. Been thinking of the soft one, where birds have nests and foxes have holes, but little Baby Jesus has no place to rest."

Lutie's face was wet with tears.

Saravette spoke the words, using the rhythm but skipping the melody.

> *"Like me, O Lord.*
> *Where's my place to rest?*
> *You holding it for me?*
> *There a manger for my head?*
> *O Lord, I need some rest."*

"I gotta say good-bye, baby girl," whispered Saravette. "You ever heard the good-bye song from the Laundry List? Bet

165

you didn't. Mama didn't like it. She didn't want to say good-bye. But I didn't give her a choice."

Saravette's voice was thick with grief and thin on notes. But she sang.

She was right. Lutie didn't know this one.

"Slow and slower still
Lord, I struggle up this hill."

Then there was silence.
And then there was nothing.

Doria held that last chord just about forever, savoring how rich and huge it was. When she lifted her hands and feet, the sound kept swirling. Even the silence was big.

And in the silence, in the motionless emptiness of the church, she knew absolutely that she was not alone. Her body lost its sophistication, its musical skills, its coordination.

She was an animal and there was a predator out there.

She did not breathe in and she did not breathe out.

She grabbed her purse, slid off the bench, leaped backward to the little side door, through which a groom came for his wedding, or the pastor for the service. She flew through a narrow back hall with a restroom, a flower room and a drinking fountain, raced up the back stairs, ran down a connecting hall, and took the elevator into the day care center.

The cleaning staff was there.

"Oh, hi!" she said, her voice brittle. "Hi, how are you?"

Two women and a man regarded her doubtfully.

"Um, I was practicing the organ?" she said. "And I got panicky. Do you think—could you walk me to my car?"

"Where you parked? Wudn't another car here when we came in."

"Out front."

"Oh. We're at the side by the playground. You know, you didn't ought to be by yourself in there at night."

She couldn't count the number of people who had told her that. They were right.

◦

Aunt Tamika came out of the kitchen. "Lutie, baby? You crying?" She rushed to the sofa, dropped beside her, held her tight and rocked her. "Tell Aunt Mika. What's wrong? I haven't heard you cry like this in years, baby girl."

Lutie handed over the cell phone. Aunt Tamika listened to Saravette's message.

Then she listened to it again and sighed. "I used to love that one. 'Where's My Place to Rest?'" Aunt Tamika sang it softly, every sweet verse, taking Baby Jesus all the way to the manger.

Lutie lay against her aunt's generous bosom. It was warm and soft. Their heartbeats merged. "I don't know the other one. 'Slow and Slower Still,'" said Lutie.

"That's because you learned the list from your grandmother, but *we* three girls learned it from *our* grandmother. Our grandmother, she sang 'Slow and Slower Still.' But my mama—your MeeMaw—she purely didn't like that one. I can't remember the verses. But it's about the hill of life, and Mabel is tired of climbing. Your MeeMaw, she wanted to believe that Mabel Painter never fell down. I don't think my mother ever sang 'Slow and Slower Still.' I haven't thought of it in years. I'm kind of touched that Saravette remembers."

How gentle her voice was. As if it wasn't only duty that

made her check on Saravette. As if she really did love her sister.

"Does Saravette mean she can't keep going either?"

"Could be. Saravette is always boxing herself in some corner. I suppose next week I better try to find her and listen to what the struggle is now. I never know if I'm loving her or enabling her. I hate that word 'enable.' It is just not a word my mama would have used."

Lutie braced herself. "Aunt Mika? The other day Saravette called me real early, and she never calls me, and I was sort of excited and proud. She begged me to come to her. She begged like she would die if I didn't. So I skipped school, and I went, and it was awful. Everything about her is awful, and the place we met was awful, and the most awful thing of all was, I didn't care. I didn't want to listen. I wanted to run."

Her aunt took a minute to recover from this news. But she didn't yell. She said sadly, "I feel that way a lot of the time. She's so hard, honey. Seeing Saravette is not rewarding, except it's the right thing to do. What did she need from you?"

"She didn't tell me. But she said she's broken all the commandments now. It was a throwaway sentence. I don't know if she knew what she was saying. But I knew. One of those commandments is 'Thou shalt not kill.' Oh, Aunt Tamika, all I can think of is *Did she? Did she kill?*"

Lutie's full weight pressed on her aunt, like a toddler falling asleep. She felt her aunt's muscles tighten, felt the stillness of her lungs, felt the shudder of those lungs filling at last. But Aunt Tamika said nothing.

Lutie sat up straight. "She did kill somebody, didn't she? And you know who."

Tamika dusted herself off and stood. "I got to stir the sauce. Probably burned by now. That's just Saravette's way of talking. She could always get a person's attention. She got yours. Well, I know you don't like salmon. And you think asparagus is disgusting because it makes your pee smell funny. So what do you want to have? The refrigerator is spilling over. You name it, we'll cook it."

"If my mother murdered somebody, I need to know."

Uncle Dean was standing motionless under the arch that separated the kitchen from the family room. He held a platter of grilled salmon. It was tilting dangerously but he seemed not to notice.

Lutie clicked on her cell. She did not often play one aunt against the other, but it was time.

Aunt Grace picked up on the second ring. "Hey, girl."

"Aunt Grace, I know Saravette killed somebody. Who was it?"

The aunt in the room and the aunt on the phone were silent.

Uncle Dean said, "Lutie, Saravette could have done a thousand bad things that we don't know about and it's not helpful to guess."

"How do you know?" demanded Aunt Grace over the phone.

"Saravette told me Thursday. When I cut school."

"You *saw* Saravette?" screamed Aunt Grace. "This wasn't over the phone?"

"Lutie, believing anything Saravette says is fatal," said Uncle Dean.

"I agree. Saravette caused a fatality. She's my mother. I want to know who she killed."

⟳

Doria used the automatic garage-door opener clipped to the visor. On went the interior garage lights and up went the door. She drove in, cut the engine and shut the garage doors behind

169

her. The lights stayed on in their watchful way, giving her a full two minutes to get inside the house before they went out.

The house was still empty.

The night would stretch on forever and tomorrow morning she would get up and drive into the city, and play two Sunday services at St. Bartholomew's. Many adults would compliment her and many teenagers would walk past.

Her cell phone rang.

It would be her parents, checking on her.

She was dutiful. She answered.

"Dore? It's me, Nell."

"Nell," said Doria, feeling disoriented.

"I was just thinking that we haven't talked in about a hundred years. I miss you."

Still standing in the archway, losing his grip on the salmon, Uncle Dean said, "I know. We'll order pizza. Lutie, you love pizza."

On the far side of town, Aunt Grace shouted into the phone and Lutie's ear. "Let me talk to Mika!"

Aunt Tamika corrected the tilt of the salmon platter. "Lutie, your uncle is right. We cannot run around taking Saravette seriously. She's just a sad crazy junkie."

Uncle Dean and Aunt Tamika managed to get the salmon to land on the kitchen counter. Uncle Dean said, "I'm usually very careful about fat intake, but let's indulge. I'll refrigerate the salmon. Lutie, what do you want on your pizza?"

Lutie screamed into the phone. "Aunt Grace! Who did Saravette kill?"

Uncle Dean said he really wanted sausage; it'd been far too long since he'd had sausage. Caramelized onions. Maybe bacon. Definitely mushrooms.

Aunt Grace screamed that nobody was to say a word until she got there. If it had to be told, they all had to tell it. But she was opposed to the idea and felt Tamika had mishandled everything.

Aunt Tamika snatched the phone out of Lutie's hands and said she had handled everything just fine. It was Saravette who'd screwed up, the way she always did, slicing apart other people's lives without giving it a thought.

"No, I'll pick up the pizzas," said Uncle Dean into his own phone, although he hated to pick up pizza. The whole point of ordering pizza was that they delivered it.

He wants to get out of here, thought Lutie.

Next to her, Aunt Tamika was crying. From Lutie's cell phone came Aunt Grace's voice, and Lutie suddenly grasped that her aunt was already on the way over, which was amazing and rather frightening. How fast was she driving? Aunt Grace! Who lobbied for laws to prevent people from talking on cell phones while they drove!

"Well, I'm off!" said her uncle, as if he planned to fly to Europe and would see them in a few weeks.

Aunt Grace was shouting, "Put Mika on the phone. Ask her should we have Veola come over?"

They all know, thought Lutie. They're all in on it. My aunts, my uncle, my pastor. They all know.

So three things are true.

My mother is Saravette.

Saravette is a murderer.

I am the daughter of a murderer.

11

There was a song on the Laundry List so rhythmic that Lutie couldn't sing it standing still. Not that Lutie was a standing-still singer. She was a swaying singer, a space-taking singer. But for this song, she was a stomp singer.

> *What you doing?*
> *Where you be?*
> *Come to me, God!*
>
> *I'm on my knees, God.*
> *Please, please, God!*
> *Come to me, God.*

Psalm 13 cried out like that. Lutie had never cared for the dark psalms, the down psalms. Now she knew what the psalmist knew.

I'm on my knees, God, thought Lutie. Come to me, God. Saravette really did keep a list and check it off, one by one. And she's my mother.

Aunt Grace flung herself into the house and then stopped right inside the door, like a delivery. She did not rush over to Lutie. There was no hugging or kissing or reassuring. She and her sister Tamika stared at each other, stealing little glances at Lutie.

"So?" said Lutie unpleasantly. "Who did she kill? And when? And why?"

Aunt Tamika's beautiful bulk sagged and became fat and failure.

Aunt Grace, who could control five long lines of frustrated patrons, two new employees, a broken fax and six ringing phones without missing a beat, made it to a chair. A stiff wooden chair that nobody ever sat in, set against the wall for symmetry. She perched on the edge, as if she planned to sprint away at any moment.

Aunt Tamika just shook her head.

It was Aunt Grace who finally spoke. "Not long after you were born, Saravette handed you to her mama and she left. She wanted to have fun. Babies get in the way when you're fifteen and fun means parties and cars and boys and dancing. She'd come by now and then, pick you up and cuddle you, maybe bring you a toy. But she wouldn't stay. I was away at college and Mika, she was a senior in high school, and we were busy. We were no help to Saravette and we were no help to Mama. Life was rich. You were maybe two years old when Saravette and your MeeMaw had a terrible fight and Saravette left for good. We'd hear that she was in Atlanta or Miami or Myrtle Beach, but we didn't know. We didn't hear from her."

How little information Lutie really had about Saravette. She had not even known—or even wondered!—how old Saravette had been when she was born. Oh, poor MeeMaw. Standing on the porch, clinging to the post, crying out in the

173

night. How she must have regretted that fight, no matter who had been right. *Be you still alive? Be you coming home?*

But Lutie, growing up, had known only love and discipline and great food. Had never caught a glimpse of heartache.

"And then one day," Aunt Grace said heavily, "Saravette came back to town. It was just awful to see what had become of her. Saravette was the beautiful one, the brilliant one. She threw it all away. I could never understand. I'm not beautiful and I'm not brilliant, but I wanted so much to make something of my life and I worked so hard! And my sister, who could have done anything, she threw herself away like trash."

"Why?" asked Lutie.

"If I could answer that, I could save the world. Why do people throw away what's good in them and keep what's bad?"

Lutie thought of Train, who had thrown away what was good in him, and now he stood around himself, like a little gang of one, admiring what was wrong in him. His idol was a brother in prison. Who had Saravette idolized? Whose track had she followed?

Aunt Grace seemed to fold, like an old newspaper that had been left out in the rain.

Aunt Tamika took her turn. In a fake upbeat voice, she said, "Your MeeMaw loved you so. She always wanted grandchildren and she was so proud of her grandbaby Lutie. She made us call her MeeMaw too, so you wouldn't get confused. There was nothing your MeeMaw liked more than photographs of you and her. On the porch, in church, getting groceries, washing the car, picking flowers, shelling peas."

The aunts detoured into MeeMaw stories. Lutie thought that soon they would drag out the old photo albums, and the three of them would sit together on this big long sofa and laugh and talk about old times. And maybe that was for the best. How much detail did Lutie really want? Whatever the

174

truth was, Lutie would find herself tarred with Saravette's crimes, a seabird in an oil spill.

"I remember that it was March Madness," said Aunt Tamika. "You were going to sleep here at our house, Lutie, so you and your uncle Dean could watch Carolina play in the Final Four, and you could yell and cheer. You had a brand-new sleeping bag for the sleepover. You phoned me off and on all day to let me know what you had packed in your overnight bag. You couldn't decide if you wanted to sleep in front of the TV or go upstairs to the bedroom you and I had decorated. I drove over to MeeMaw's to get you. You and MeeMaw were waiting on the porch. It was chilly. You were wearing a fleece jacket."

That sleeping bag had been covered with rainbows. The hoodie had been lime green. The overnight bag had been an old airline carry-on from when Aunt Grace flew back and forth to college. Bright red, with scuff marks that wouldn't come out. Lutie remembered standing on the porch, waiting for Aunt Tamika to drive up so she could go watch basketball with Uncle Dean, the world's best sports-watching companion, whose running commentary would be a hundred times more exciting and interesting than the TV crew's.

While they waited for Aunt Tamika, MeeMaw had been singing, of course, but not from the Laundry List. She had been singing her favorite hymn: "The Ninety and Nine." It was a ballad, unusual for a hymn. Ninety and nine sheep were safe in the fold, but one was lost on the mountain, far from the gates of gold. The Lord set out to find his lost sheep, and what a struggle he had on that rough mountain. He got hurt, but he kept going. Finally, the angels heard him cry. "Rejoice! I have found my sheep!" Lutie smiled at the memory of MeeMaw singing.

Aunt Grace covered her eyes.

Aunt Tamika stood up, but not tall. She hung there like an old dishrag. "So I brought you here," she said, waving around the room. "You and your uncle Dean were calling the coach a bad name and clutching each other in panic because it was just possible that we would lose. And the phone rang." Aunt Tamika looked shocked, as if phones didn't normally ring. Her head turned woodenly toward the archway and the kitchen beyond. She stared at the phone hanging on the kitchen wall, its curly cord dangling. It wasn't in use, since Aunt Tamika and Uncle Dean no longer had a landline. "You didn't hear it ring," said Aunt Tamika, in a trembly voice. "Uncle Dean didn't hear it ring." There was a pause and then she said sadly, "I heard it ring."

Aunt Grace was hugging herself, tightening her arms around her chest. She hunched down, making a box of herself.

"It was Miss Veola," said Aunt Tamika. "Miss Veola was your MeeMaw's best friend," she said, as if Lutie might have forgotten. "Eunice and Veola, they'd been friends forever. Founded a church together. Ran committees and gardened and shopped and ate out." She shook her head. "You finish, Grace," she whispered.

Aunt Grace unfolded herself. Released her arms. Lifted her chin. Drew a shaky breath. She said, "Saravette had been in town a few days by then. We wouldn't let her see you. We wouldn't let you see her. It was too awful. What drugs can do to a person. Anyway, Miss Veola got a call. Turned out Saravette had dropped in at MeeMaw's that night, when you were over here watching basketball with Dean. Saravette phoned Veola from MeeMaw's house. *Come quick,* she said, *I need you.* So Veola hurried over."

By day, Miss Veola would have walked. Like Eunice Painter, she loved the woods and the brook and the meadow

176

But after dark, she would have driven her Cadillac. Lutie imagined the big shiny car coming up the narrow drive. She imagined the headlights illuminating the little house and Miss Veola parking.

"MeeMaw was lying on the ground by the porch. She was dead. Saravette kept saying, 'I didn't mean to. She got me so mad. I just gave her a push. I didn't know she'd fall! It's only two steps!'"

Lutie saw the flat of Saravette's hand, felt it flex, felt the strength of the arm and body shoving it forward.

She saw MeeMaw falling backward, hitting the ground. Seeing the stars above one last time and then departing to be among them.

If you believed in stars.

If you believed in anything, once you found out that a daughter could kill her own mother.

Lutie was up off the sofa and screaming. "Why are you telling me this? You shouldn't be telling me! I don't want to know! I hate you!" She looked around for something to smash and ruin.

"We had to tell you," said Aunt Grace. "Or else Saravette would. She's building up to it. And if you went once to see Saravette without us, you might go a second time. You know we would never have let you go into the city last week! When Saravette is using, and she gets angry, and somebody's in her way, now you know what she can do."

Lutie took refuge behind the piano. It was a pretty little blond wood spinet rented for Lutie's piano lessons, but Lutie never got around to taking any. "I don't know how you can go near Saravette at all! You buy her cell phones and you chat away with her and you drive around and check up on her and all along, you knew. She killed your mother!"

Probably Saravette had been facing her mother when she put out her hands and shoved. Probably the last eyes into which Eunice Painter looked were her baby girl's.

One burst of temper, and one life was over and one life was ruined.

MeeMaw, prayed Lutie, I hope you didn't know.

After a long time, Lutie whispered, "And then what happened?"

"For a year or so," said Aunt Grace, "Saravette called me and Tamika and Veola all the time. I don't know what they said, but I said terrible things. She must have wanted to hear me scream and swear because she called me the most. Couple of times, she tried to kill herself, but drugs can't be relied on, even for death. But in the end, Lutie, I went to find her. She's my sister. Mama would have wanted us to cherish each other, no matter what. Sometimes I can and sometimes I can't."

"How come the police didn't arrest her?"

"Because your aunts and your preacher didn't tell anybody," said Uncle Dean.

Lutie had forgotten about her uncle. She had not heard him return. Now she smelled pizza: the unmistakable call of tomato sauce and oregano.

"Preachers know death," said Aunt Tamika. "They're always at hospitals and hospices and bedsides and funeral homes. Miss Veola knew that her dear friend Eunice was gone. Veola didn't want Eunice remembered as the woman killed by her own baby girl. She wanted Eunice remembered for her love and charity, her church work and garden and cooking and laughter and, above all, her singing. The beautiful voice that would float out over Chalk so that people would stop where they were and listen and know God."

Lutie could not stand all these digressions. "Okay, but that night? What happened that night?"

"Dean stayed here with you, while Grace and I hurried to Mama's. Saravette kept saying it was an accident, but what's accidental about a push? Veola sent Saravette packing. When she was gone, we called the ambulance. We said we hadn't heard from MeeMaw and when we came over, we found her lying there. Nobody ever asked any questions, so none of us had to lie."

Uncle Dean said, "I thought they were wrong. I thought Saravette's best hope was jail and a drug program. But they didn't want you to know either, Lutie. And now you know after all and we didn't save you from anything."

Lutie felt as if she were watching one or two frames of a long cruel movie. She needed more visuals. "How did you send Saravette packing? Did she have a car?"

"She walked through the woods and over the creek and into Chalk, and what she did next, I couldn't say. I didn't care."

Lutie knew those woods. She knew every tree and rock. She imagined Saravette wading through Peter Creek, stumbling into Chalk, hoping to hitch a ride somewhere. Anywhere.

Tamika said, "Saravette phoned a few days after that. She was in Atlanta. I don't know how she got there. At the funeral people said, 'Where's Saravette?' And we said, 'She's hard to reach.' And they said, 'Poor Eunice. That girl broke her heart.' Which was true. Broke her neck as well."

What if these terrible images never left Lutie's mind? What if they hung there, playing themselves like melodies from the Laundry List? What if the only song in her soul was "Be You Still Alive?"?

"That message Saravette left on your phone, Lutie?" said Aunt Grace. "She sounds drunk as a skunk to me. I don't even give her credit for saying she's sorry. I think when she spreads the story around, she's handing some off to you, which leaves less for her to bear and that's all the phone call is. Making it easier on herself."

Neither Tamika nor Grace had said, "I forgave Saravette." Because who could?

⟲

Nell chattered on, as if she'd been texting and tweeting and messaging so much that her voice needed to flex. She was a fountain of gossip. It was comforting, and yet remote. Doria had the sensation of paging through some old yearbook, squinting to remember old acquaintances. How brisk Nell sounded compared to the leisurely pace of speaking in Court Hill.

"Now, I promised Steph that the moment you and I wrap up, you'll call her," said Nell. "I mean, we keep saying, we've got to call Dore. And then we don't get to it."

Because you have better things to do, thought Doria. But at least Steph is calling now. I haven't actually lost my friends. I'm just out of sight.

"So I'm on my computer in my bedroom," said Nell, "and I'm looking at the Court Hill High website. Point people out to me."

Doria started with the basketball team, and Azure Lee, its captain.

Nell was impressed. "She lives on your street? Wow. Amazing hair. She must have a thousand braids. She is stunning."

Then the swim team, and Pierce.

"He's gorgeous! And he lives down the street too? Why are you on the phone with me? You should be beating down his door!"

They worked through Rebecca and Jenny, while Doria

threw in a brief mention of graduating early, and then offered Kelvin, like dessert. She admitted that Kelvin, although perfect, was not looking her way. But reality had not dimmed her crush. Doria would even take up baking for Kelvin.

A thousand miles apart, the girls studied Kelvin's Facebook page.

"He does look like a person who would enjoy cookies," said Nell.

"I don't know how to present them," said Doria. "Do I bake enough cookies for the whole chorus and he'll taste one and come up afterward? Or just grab him in the hall and hand him a ribbon-wrapped paper plate?"

"Tricky," agreed Nell.

"Here's something even trickier." Doria told her about the lost songs, and Mr. Gregg and Professor Durham. "I understand wanting to take the songs. I wanted to take them myself, and send them to colleges as my audition tape for music school."

"I thought you were going into premed," said Nell.

"Whatever. We're talking about stealing songs, Nell."

"No, we aren't. It isn't stealing. Lutie doesn't have a copyright. She doesn't even have a recording."

"But her grandmother's grandmother wrote them."

"I doubt it," said Nell. "Apparently that whole community did laundry. Must have done it outdoors. Probably did it together, like picking peaches or something. I bet they were group songs. But tell me more about graduating early. It's a good idea. You'll come back up here for college and we'll see each other more."

"I was thinking of the University of Texas. They call it by its initials—UT. There are almost fifty thousand students there. Can you imagine?"

"I'm sure Texas is a fine place," said Nell, in the voice of one who doesn't think so at all, "but your friends are here. Now let's get back to Pierce. He has possibilities."

"He's adorable. But he's not the one I have a crush on."

"So? Is he in that Youth Group?"

"Technically, I think. But he wasn't there last week."

"Text him. See if he's going this week. See if you can ride with him."

"Nell, I ruined it when they found out I'm studying physics on my own. He and Azure Lee fled."

"He's had time to think about it now," said Nell, "and he's impressed."

"Where did you get that from?"

"Wishful thinking," said Nell. "Listen, it was good to hear your voice," she said, moving into wrap-up mode. "Toughen up down there. Or lighten up. I can't quite tell."

And then she was gone. The silence in the house felt permanent. The whole conversation took on a minor-key sound, the sound of somebody making an effort.

Doria looked up Pierce's cell phone number on a neighborhood watch list and texted him before she could think better of it.

Went to YG at First Meth last wk. U going this Sunday?

A text message was dry and casual. All Pierce had to do was write back one word. It would probably be no, and that would be that.

Next she texted Lutie. *I have the chords. Meet and play the Laundry List?*

The thought of such a duet put Doria in a key-of-C mood. C was a sunshine key. A key that woke up knowing it was going to be a good day.

Uncle Dean, Aunt Tamika, Aunt Grace and Lutie were sitting at the table watching pizza congeal. A hot pizza is beautiful but a cold one is a sorry sight.

"What if," said Lutie, "the professor looks for Saravette, and she says to him, 'I broke all the commandments,' and he says, 'Really? Who did you kill?' . . . and she tells him?"

"Never going to happen," said Uncle Dean. "If he finds Saravette—and let me tell you, that's a task—he'd see a pathetic junkie. I don't think he'd listen to a word she says. Even a cop wouldn't take Saravette seriously. And if she said out loud and direct, 'I killed my mama,' everybody would say, 'You sure did, girl. Broke her heart six ways to Sunday.'"

And all I care about, thought Lutie, is what people will think of me. That would break MeeMaw's heart six ways to Sunday, too.

Sunday

Doria goes for the gold.
Jesus steps on Lutie's toes.
Pierce calls the police.

12

Eight minutes before the church service began, Doria Bell sat on the organ bench in St. Bartholomew's.

She had chosen a quiet weaving fugue that was six minutes long. But she was not in the mood for an intellectual piece. She was in a show-off, knock-their-socks-off mood.

The chances were about one in two hundred fifty (the number of people here today) that anybody would know whether she played the piece printed in the bulletin. The choir director might. But during the prelude, he was out in the hall, arranging the choir for the processional. For hundreds of years, grown-ups had been processing on the first hymn, and still they couldn't figure out where to stand.

The organ at First Methodist might be big and lusty, but the one here at St. Bartholomew's was massive. Doria whipped out her Vierne symphony, opened the swell pedals, pulled out all the stops and plunged into the rocket charge of the sixth movement.

The whole church practically had a heart attack.

A full organ at full volume was in total control. Her

audience couldn't think, move or talk. She owned these people.

Doria grinned.

She went for the gold, whipping the page turns, racing through the measures.

She held the last chord approximately forever and then lifted her hands with a flourish. There was utter silence, the audience still inside the music, even when it stopped.

And then they applauded.

This was not a church where people clapped. But now they did, in the exhilarated way of people who want to be part of the action and take it home with them.

They were glad they had paid half a million dollars for this instrument, thrilled that they had just heard every sound it had to give. They had not yet worshipped and neither had she, but they were stirred now, and ready.

Reverend Warren stood up and walked to the pulpit. "That, my friends, was the Word of God."

⟳

Sunday morning, Lutie slept as if she were anesthetized. Aunt Tamika had to shake her awake. Lutie was supposed to sing a solo, so Aunt Tamika dragged her to church and dropped her off. Nobody else was there yet.

"I don't want to sing," Lutie told Miss Veola. "I don't have enough air." Lutie felt as if her skin had turned transparent, and anybody could see right through her and pull out the secret of Eunice Painter's death, like a book on a shelf, and read the details.

"I cannot believe Mika and Grace told you about that terrible night," said Miss Veola. She looked old and crumpled. "It's a burden I do not want you carrying. Did you save Saravette's phone message? May I hear it too?"

188

Lutie handed over her cell.

Miss Veola listened to Saravette's maudlin speech. She gripped the back of the nearest pew, and slowly lowered herself onto the velvet cushion. "I feel like Saravette. Slow and slower still."

Miss Veola did not look like a woman who could lead a church service.

It dawned on Lutie that even Miss Veola needed prayer. Lutie took her pastor's hand. "Jesus, Miss Veola wants to be the shepherd, and run out in the night on the mountain and save Saravette. But first she has to be the shepherd here and speak to her own flock. You give her strength to get through the morning, Lord."

Praying, Lutie often felt as if she were writing a letter, and instead of saying amen, she wanted to sign off, "Love, Lutie." So she looked up, way up, and said, "Love, Lutie."

The sermon always came toward the end of the service. At St. Bartholomew's, it lasted about fifteen minutes. Doria usually rested up from what she had already played, listened to a paragraph or so, and then thought about what she would play next: the final hymn, the choral Amen and the postlude.

But Reverend Warren's first sentence grabbed her.

"What stuff do you love?" he said eagerly, already basking in the stuff he loved. "Me, I'm a country boy. I love my tractor. I love my pickup truck. And when I get home, wow, do I love my wife's cooking." He patted his gut, and the congregation, many of whom sported a similarly ample gut, laughed with him.

"But stuff doesn't last," he said regretfully. "My tractor will rust. And food—for sure, in our house, it doesn't last long. Last church I preached at, over to the coast, beautiful building, very old, it lasted through the Civil War. It stood firm through hurricanes and street riots. But now it's got termites. Bugs are gonna get it in the end. It's just stuff and it won't last. And our bodies, they wear out, and then we pass on. Stuff doesn't last, even us."

Music lasts, thought Doria. If you print it, and record it, and sing it for the next generation.

"The Bible tells us that only three things last: faith, hope and love. But there's a problem. We leave all three of those behind on this earth when we die. Faith, hope and love stay here only if we give them away. That's your job this week. Faith, hope and love. Give 'em away, as much as you can, to every person you can."

Lutie thought Miss Veola would never wrap up her sermon. Five times already Lutie had thought she was at the end, and five times Miss Veola had waded into another topic. Even this congregation, who came ready to sit for a long while, was itchy.

"I used to think," said Miss Veola, "that what people want most is to be loved, and to love in return. I've had to change my mind. People want to be noticed. It's similar to being loved, but it doesn't require emotion or commitment. You just stand there and make sure people see you. 'Look at me!' screams the person on the reality show. 'Listen to me!' sings the person in the music contest. But I say, Look at God. Listen to him."

"Amen," called a few worshippers.

"And Amen," agreed Miss Veola.

During coffee hour, Lutie hid out in a Sunday-school room. She had known these people all her life, but she didn't want any part of them today.

It took forever for the last car to drive off.

Lutie came out of hiding and found Miss Veola sitting on

the church steps in the shade. Lutie sat beside her. The pastor always gave her a ride home on Sundays.

They sat together, postponing cleanup in the sanctuary. There was a janitor, of course, but he did not meet Miss Veola's standards. He always wanted to wait until Monday, but Miss Veola could not lock up her church unless it was in pristine condition.

They said nothing. Miss Veola had probably used every word she possessed in her sermon and Lutie still didn't have enough air.

St. Bartholomew's had two services, at nine and eleven. It was one reason why Doria's parents rarely came. Long drive, long morning. Instead, Doria would take her mother's Honda and go on her own. After the second service, she headed home. She was tired. Even the car was tired. It was a slow trip.

Faith, hope and love. Give 'em away, as much as you can, to every person you can.

But what if people weren't interested?

She hadn't heard from Pierce. Did she have the energy to go to that Youth Group by herself? Jenny and Rebecca might be there. Maybe this time they would just have fun, no volunteer requests or preaching.

She hadn't heard from Lutie, either.

The Bells always had Sunday dinner at a restaurant in the country with an amazing buffet. Even Doria, a picky eater to the max, could find seconds and thirds there. It was a busy noisy anonymous place, and perfect for talking from the heart. So much was happening in her life and she had shared so little. It wouldn't be faith, hope or love that she'd give her parents. It would be detail. That was what they wanted, to be part of her world. That was what she had withheld.

She reached Tenth Street. On her left, largely hidden by oaks and pines, was Chalk. And on her right was a small brick church. Veola Mixton, Pastor said the sign. Church was over. The gravel parking lot was mostly empty. Doria slowed down to see if she could spot anything pink but she couldn't.

On the church steps sat two people.

Lutie and Miss Veola.

∽

A car hovered in the road. Its signal light blinked as it turned slowly into the church lot. Who would show up now? It was dinnertime. Lutie did not recognize the car. She peered at the driver.

Doria Bell.

I can't stand it, thought Lutie. I'm too busy knowing what I know.

Doria had texted that she had chosen chords for the Laundry List. Chords would change the songs. They'd be more typical, more marketable. But diluted. And with chords and a piano, musicologists would never hear the real song. They would never see Mabel and her sweat and the harsh soap and the hot iron. They would hear the List like anything else that played on a radio.

Should the songs be sung only the way Mabel had sung them?

Should Lutie and Doria give the Laundry List a new shape and a new audience?

Or should Lutie allow the songs to lapse and vanish into silence, like dead languages?

I'm sick of the Laundry List, she thought. "Lord," said Lutie out loud, "make Doria evaporate."

"Jesus," said Miss Veola sharply, "step on Lutie's toes."

Lutie straightened her legs, admiring her slender ankles and the nicely shaped toes peeking out of her open-toed heels. "Ouch. Jesus has heavy shoes."

"He's wearing sandals," corrected Miss Veola. "And it's important to remember that you are not worthy even to tighten his sandal strap."

"Could you give it a rest already?" said Lutie.

Doria leaned out the driver's-side window. "Good morning. Is this a good time?"

"It is," said Lutie. "Jesus just showed up. He's been stepping on my toes."

"That doesn't sound like him," said Doria.

"He only does it by special request. Want to see our church? Bet it's not the same as St. Bartholomew's."

⌒

No wonder they called it the pink church.

The interior was no soft gentle pastel. It was a pink that screamed, a pink that assaulted the eyes. Gaudy, shocking, neon pink. As loud as a rock band in a stadium.

Miss Veola had chosen this? *Liked* it? Thought it was appropriate?

Miss Veola was laughing at Doria's expression. "Jesus wasn't background," she explained. "He didn't blend. So I don't either."

"Where I come from, churches are all white," said Doria.

"No duh," said Miss Veola.

Doria blushed. "I meant the paint. I thought when you said pink, it would be some sweet gentle rose."

"Sugar, when you play the organ, are you always a sweet gentle rose?"

"I play it all on all there is."

"My philosophy of life, honey. Play it all on all there is."

Doria walked slowly down the aisle toward the altar, which was a plain table, the wood gleaming from years of polish. The chancel was raised a few steps, and the lower step was carpeted, so people could kneel and pray. Even the carpet was pink.

A starched and ironed white cloth ran down the middle of the altar. There were candlesticks, a cross, offertory plates and a vacuum cleaner resting against the rail. It looked like a painting, the gentle oddity of the cleaning equipment keeping the scene earthbound.

On the floor and flanking the altar were instruments: percussion, keyboard, speakers and a battered brown baby grand, which looked as if kids stood around kicking the piano legs during the children's sermon. She hoped it was better tuned than it looked. Few things bothered her more than a badly tuned piano. Just last week, she had had to tell Mr. Gregg to tune his piano or she was history.

"I know you're an organist, not a pianist, Doria," called Miss Veola, "but I just want to sit back here and listen while you fill this room with music. Play anything."

⤶

Lutie loved this church.

Miss Veola had not physically built the building. She had built it spiritually. Taken a fading congregation and whipped it into excitement and commitment.

But the shouting pink of the old walls and the quieter pink of the low ceiling, the polished dark wood of its sturdy altar rail—on which rickety old folks hauled themselves up off their knees—how could that be equaled by the skinny stage of a failed movie theater?

Could you really worship God anywhere?

Or did the church itself need soul?

What would happen to the years and years of worship that had taken place here?

Oh, stop being a drama queen, Lutie ordered herself. Pastor Craig's congregation is moving in. Worship won't miss a beat.

She leaned against Miss Veola and thought of Saravette and the meaning of friendship and forgiveness, and Jesus standing on her toes.

The best thing about church was that it sanctioned profound thoughts. In school, in Chalk, at the mall, on the phone, being profound felt silly. But at church, it lay waiting, deep and beautiful.

At the chancel, Doria's fingers moved over the keyboard, playing a cloudy wash of chords, like waves coming ashore at the beach. Deep inside the notes, Lutie began to hear "Mama, You Sleep." On and on rolled the lullaby. *All those worries— leave 'em on the porch.*

But a porch, especially that porch, where MeeMaw had sung that song and had her last conversation with Saravette, was no longer a place Lutie wanted to be.

13

G *ot the car,* Pierce texted.

Doria wanted to answer, *Great! Wow! I can't believe you wrote back! You're driving? I get to sit in front with you? You're not afraid to show up with me?*

Instead she wrote, *What time?*

Now would be good, he replied.

"I'm going to Youth Group with Pierce," she said casually to her parents.

They were repainting their bathroom. The builders had chosen eggshell walls and navy trim. Her mom had picked out buttercup walls with white trim. Dad had the prisoner look of a man who could think of forty-seven things he'd rather be doing. But he just grinned at his daughter. Mom was too busy taping to look up. "Enjoy," she said vaguely.

Pierce was already tapping his horn. Doria flew to the curb and got in the car.

"My mom is so happy I'm doing this," he said. "My dad can't believe I'm doing it. We were watching football."

"Who's playing?"

"Doria, do you even know a football from a basketball?"

"Almost."

He turned onto Hill Street. "What's Youth Group doing tonight?" he asked. "I might have too much homework if there are sermons or lectures. We might have to leave early."

"There was a visiting sermonist last week, so probably this week is non-sermon."

"Is that a word? Sermonist?"

"Probably not."

"I like it, though," said Pierce. "A sermonist. One who sermons. Probably a tedious person." He handed her his phone. It was new and sleek, with much more capability than her own. She was jealous. "Look up First Methodist," he ordered.

I could buy a phone like this, she thought. I have lots of money. What am I saving it for, anyway, if not a great phone?

She clicked onto First Methodist's site and then on the link for the Youth Group page. "Tonight is fried chicken and volleyball. This is not good. I don't volley."

Pierce was laughing. "A little volleying will offset some of that online physics. Every time I think of that I start laughing."

"What's the funny part?"

"I just can't get an image of it. You curling up in front of the computer for a physics lecture."

It turned out that prior to volleyball, Youth Group had to do something religious. Jenny's mother had been drafted, since everybody else was busy. The poor woman had decided to lead thirty teenagers in song. She started with an old Sunday-school ditty, "This Little Light of Mine."

The kids moaned. Maybe a quarter of them gave it a whirl.

"This little light of mine,
I'm gonna let it shine."

Doria said, "The trouble with this song is nobody wants to be a little light. Everybody wants to be a spotlight, or have one."

"I'm sure that's not a nice way to think," said Jenny's mother, who clearly knew nothing about her daughter.

"Doria's right," said Rebecca. "We don't want to be tidy little candles in a small town on a Sunday afternoon. We want to shine on the world's stage."

It was one of those moments when nobody was shy and everybody could admit the truth: they wanted to be special and they wanted the world to acknowledge it. Kid after kid confessed to the kind of stardom he or she hoped for.

Pierce was last. "I think I'm standard issue. I don't see myself achieving stardom. But I'm okay with that."

How amazing that Pierce could think of himself as standard issue.

"Think of Train, though," said Jenny. "He'll never be a star. He'll never even be an extra. He won't even get tickets to the show. I think it's actually making him crazy."

Evan said, "I agree with you. Train is looking for a spotlight. Or maybe DeRade ordered him to find the spotlight. But he can't find it. Or doesn't have the guts."

"Really?" said Michael. "I think Train has guts. And I also think he's crazy. He's ready to burst. He'll bring guns or hand grenades to school."

Pierce was shocked. "Do you mean that?"

"He's frantic," said Michael. "Pulsing. Like a warning light."

"He's ready," agreed Evan. "But for what, exactly? I don't agree that he'd bring guns or grenades to school."

"I like Train," protested Doria. "He's perfectly nice whenever we chat."

"Train chats?" said Rebecca. "'Chat' is the last word I would choose when that creepy guy stares with those dead eyes."

Pierce was on his cell phone. "Dad? There's sort of a feeling here that Train Greene might be ready to bring guns to school."

"Hey! Don't use my name!" said Michael.

"Why's he calling his father?" asked Jenny.

"His daddy's a homicide cop," said Michael. "Like we need Train to know we're talking about him. Last time somebody ratted on a Greene brother, he lost an eye."

"I'm not naming names," Pierce told them. "No, Dad," he said into the phone, "just kids in Youth Group."

Jenny's mother butted in. "Doria, I understand that you took advantage of the opportunity offered last Sunday to volunteer in our community. Would you tell us whether the charity involving meal delivery in Chalk seems worth our money and time?"

"It was worth *my* time. A hundredfold. But on the other hand, a visiting professor was not impressed."

"Tell us," said Rebecca. "I've never even been in Chalk. It's supposed to be so dangerous."

Doria told them about her afternoon. She talked for so long that when she looked at the time, she blushed.

"So it isn't dangerous," said Rebecca.

"Miss Kendra was careful. She kept her eye on me and twice said to stay next to the Explorer. But everybody was nice and smiling. Train even found my car keys that I dropped and brought them to me."

"Train hasn't done a thoughtful thing since he stopped being Cliff," said Pierce. "And this isn't the first time there's been interest in your keys. What exactly happened, Doria?"

"Are you going to tell your father about that, too?"

"Doria, it's better to prevent murders than solve them."

"Who's talking about murder?" demanded Rebecca.

"I am," said Pierce. "Train and DeRade blinded a kid. If Train is ready to take a step up, it would be murder."

"They didn't completely blind Nate," Jenny pointed out. "He lost one eye, not both."

"Just an oversight," said Pierce. "Train won't get it wrong next time. So are we going to play volleyball or just hang around talking about psychopaths?"

Monday

Lutie skips school.
Train corners Kelvin.
Death comes.

14

Monday morning Lutie woke up feeling separated from the Lutie she had been the previous sixteen years. That Lutie was innocent and stupid.

This Lutie was afraid of being among the other kids. The threads that knit her to her friends and classmates had unraveled. She was separate; she would always be separate. Her family secret was the worst secret there could ever be.

Doria was separate from most people most of the time. How did she get up and face the world every morning with that burden?

"You have to go to school," said Aunt Tamika. "I'll drive you. The minute you get there, this feeling will diminish. You'll be busy, school will be full of demands and you'll start forgetting."

Forget that her mother had murdered her grandmother?

Lutie couldn't find anything to wear. Usually getting dressed was a highlight of her day. She often went to sleep wrestling with the delightful decision of choosing tomorrow's outfit.

Today Aunt Tamika picked out her clothes. Lutie didn't

even argue. Then Aunt Tamika drove her up the long curved drop-off lane at Court Hill High and Lutie just could not get that car door open.

"Don't be so melodramatic," said Aunt Tamika. "Nothing has changed. It's just that you know more. Now, you text me all day long. At lunch, Grace and I are taking a few hours off and we'll try to find Saravette."

What for? Why had they ever tried to find Saravette? Why on earth did they want to find her now? Lutie wanted to throw up just thinking of her.

"I can't tell from her message if she was drunk, or sick, cornered by something else she's done, or mixed up with some deal gone bad," said her aunt. "Or if she just felt weepy and threw her sins at you instead of us. So we'll see if we can find her. That's our job, not yours. You be a scholar and make us proud."

When Aunt Tamika's car was out of sight, Lutie skipped school for the second time in her life and walked home.

◌

Train was summoned to the principal's office.

There was a cop car parked out in front of the high school, but that was often the case.

Didn't have to be for him.

Train thought about Saturday night, as he had edged closer to the organ. He thought about Doria, flinging herself out a door he had not seen. He thought about getting himself safely out of the church. Hadn't been easy. Two men and a woman were circling outside and kept coming back to circle some more.

Doria must have heard him, although he was sure he had not made a sound. But she couldn't have seen him. Couldn't have named him. If the police were here for him, it could not be over using a stolen church key and stalking Doria.

Court Hill High was a very easy building to leave, with all its outside doors. Train thought about walking away, shrugging about a stupid summons to the office, but he knew what DeRade would do. DeRade would swagger right in and laugh at the cops.

So Train took his time but eventually sauntered into the office.

Two cops.

He knew them both.

One was Pierce's daddy.

Train refused to cooperate. No, he wouldn't sit, he wouldn't take a soda, he wouldn't talk.

But the cops were not accusing him of anything. They were trying to be all fatherly and understanding. What was he planning, they wanted to know. How could they help?

Train had so many plans he couldn't decide where to start. The set-a-kid-on-fire plan; the slice-someone's-palms-open plan; the join-the-army-and-let-them-make-the-decisions plan.

"See," said Pierce's daddy, "you got a real special nickname. Train. I think it fits. A train is big and powerful. But it has to stay on its track. DeRade now, he followed a track went only one way. He never wanted a ticket out. He wanted a ticket straight to prison. But here's the deal. It's your train. You can choose where to get off."

Train didn't listen to sermons. Not his mother's, not Miss Veola's, and certainly not the police's. He thought of a piece Doria had played the other night. It was like arithmetic: notes as neat as long division, lined up in tidy columns. It got bigger and more complex, like going from arithmetic to algebra to calculus. He used to love arithmetic. He was failing it now, like he was failing everything, because he refused to study.

There was one thing he refused to fail.

Following DeRade's orders.

Train's cell phone rang.

The detectives got all alert.

Train looked down at his phone.

Stop, Miss·Veola had texted.

The only person besides the police who calls me, he thought. Religion and the law, they want me. Nobody else.

Anxiety and eagerness to know more infected the school. Teachers fluttered, students stomped.

The police had come for Train.

Nobody at Court Hill High knew what he had done.

Nobody doubted that he had done it.

In the cafeteria, Kelvin was sitting alone. He liked lunch and frequently took two rather than hustle back to class. His next class was Business Skills, none of which Kelvin wanted anyway.

Somebody would join him soon, and he'd chat with them, or he wouldn't, but either way he'd be content.

Kelvin dozed in a patch of sun, protected by his nice even temperature.

Train yanked out a chair and sat down at Kelvin's table. "You turn me in?"

"No."

"Then it was Pierce."

"Pierce?" Kelvin was amazed. "Lives down by Azure Lee?"

"The one."

Pierce was a swimmer, a group singularly isolated from everybody else, proudly removed from the usual sports like football, basketball and baseball. What did Pierce know about anything? Azure Lee, now—he could see Azure Lee turning in Train in a heartbeat. Azure Lee was tougher than all of them put together.

Kelvin said, "So what'd you do?"

"What makes you think I did anything?"

Kelvin raised his eyebrows. That was not DeRade talking. DeRade would have bragged about ten evil acts even if he hadn't committed one.

Train glittered, and Kelvin felt as if he could see future evil acts lining up, ready to come onstage, ready to spill blood. Train gave him a savage grin, as if he had won a contest Kelvin had not known they were competing in.

Kelvin was suddenly afraid.

⟳

Aunt Tamika called Lutie's cell.

Lutie muted the TV she was watching from Aunt Tamika's big sofa.

"We didn't find Saravette, Lutie. She's not answering her phone. Nobody at the building where she was last month has seen her. Grace went into shelters. I tried a soup kitchen."

Good, thought Lutie. Lost is the best place for her.

⟳

At four o'clock that afternoon, Doria was in yet another church. Mr. Bates's, where he was the organist and directed the choir and gave lessons.

It was a megachurch, complete with escalators to the upper tiers of seating, huge screens on which the minister could be seen from a distance, a symphonic band to supplement the organ and a professional choir. It had its own coffee shop and bookstore. It held services in Spanish and Korean, and had dedicated ministers for both those languages. It seated five thousand.

Doria told Mr. Bates about the Laundry List.

He was fascinated. "Sing the songs for me," he said.

Doria slid off the organ bench. "I think I have to stand. Lutie stands."

"Is Lutie our new measure of perfection?"

"At Court Hill High, she is." Doria stood on the edge of the massive stage, facing all those seats. Good thing they were empty. She liked an audience, but an audience that big would definitely be a test.

She sang the two songs she knew.

When she finished, Mr. Bates said, "Doria, I had no idea. Your voice is like liquid silver."

"Oh, thanks, but the songs need Lutie. She just has so much power."

"You mean volume or that her delivery is powerful?"

"Both," she said, sliding back onto the bench.

"I haven't met Professor Durham," said Mr. Bates, "but he's well known in his field. I think you should coax Lutie to work with him. The worst thing would be for the songs to get lost after all, and that could so easily happen. Lutie seems to be the only caretaker, as it were. Suppose she goes to college and gets into other stuff. She becomes a doctor or a lawyer and doesn't have time for music and loses interest in church and goes big-time into some splashy career on the West Coast and Court Hill is just a memory. Then the songs evaporate."

Doria was tired of the Laundry List. She said, "Mr. Bates, I don't want to have my church job anymore."

"No! Doria! You need it for a thousand reasons. You get to perform every week. Very few musicians have that privilege. You always have something to work for, because you always need more music. You give up your church job, then you're learning music just for your own sake, and the pressure of the world can make that too hard."

"But it's so dorky. And everybody's on my case not to practice alone in the church in the dark."

"And do you?"

"Of course I do. So do you. So does every organist. And the other thing I'm thinking of is, I'm thinking of graduating a year early."

"Don't. College is enough of a shock. You don't want to be younger than everybody else."

"You're the one who says I'm too mature for my age."

"Yeah, well, that's high school. In college, when everyone's drinking and partying and sleeping around, you have to be strong to steer clear. You need that extra year, Doria. Now, about last Sunday at St. Bartholomew's. They applauded when you did the Vierne?"

"Yes."

"Did they stand up? Was it a real ovation?"

"They're Presbyterians. They don't get that excited."

"But it's a goal," said Mr. Bates. "Get them on their feet. Now play that Vierne for me, and I want it more powerful than Lutie. I want to be forced to stand because I'm so excited."

⟡

"Dad!" said Pierce, choking on his dinner. "You talked to Train yourself?"

"Train was intimidated. If he had any plans, he won't try them now. Pass the hot sauce."

"Dad! If you intimidated him, it's even worse! Now he's got to prove that cops can't shove him around. I'm the person he'll prove it to."

Pierce's mother was beside herself. She wanted Pierce in private school, or out of state, or maybe she should leave the whole marriage and this stupid person who thought he was a law enforcement officer, but in fact was putting his own son's life and eyesight at risk!

Pierce's parents rarely argued in his presence and he liked to believe they rarely argued at all. He went into the backyard rather than be proven wrong.

Around him stretched big brick houses with their big green yards. He saw Fountain Ridge suddenly as a sort of classy prison: you could hide out here, safe in your matching sets of bushes and trees, safe among three-car garages and the weed-whacked edges of lawns. Nothing could touch you here. They didn't even have insects in Fountain Ridge, because everything was sprayed and treated.

He thought of Train, the least sprayed and treated person in Court Hill High.

Aunt Tamika got home early.

Aunt Grace got home with her.

Uncle Dean drove up at the same time.

They walked into the house together, an out-of-step trio at the wrong time of day.

"What?" said Lutie. She didn't care if they knew she'd skipped school today. They should get used to it.

Aunt Grace shook her head.

"What?" said Lutie again.

Aunt Tamika was crying.

"What?" shouted Lutie.

"Saravette," said Uncle Dean. "She's dead."

15

"The police found her," said Aunt Tamika. "She went on a binge. Drinking, drugs, pills, everything she could find. Police got her to the ER and called me. Dean and I drove as fast as we could. She had already passed."

Lutie thought of MeeMaw on the porch in the dark, singing "Be You Still Alive?"

No. Not anymore.

"She's been heading that way for a long while," said Tamika. "I don't think she minded going offstage forever. It was a terrible death in a terrible place, but one good thing." Aunt Tamika smiled shakily at Lutie. "She told the person she loved good-bye and I'm sorry."

"Me?"

"You."

"But if she loved me . . ."

"Saravette was desperate all her life, Lutie. Desperate for what, I never knew. She couldn't be satisfied with anything. She couldn't stick to anything. She couldn't work hard for anything. She could only thrash around."

"But when she was sober and straight, Lutie," said Uncle Dean, "she was a precious gem."

"How often was she sober and straight?" asked Lutie.

There was a pause. "Actually, I never saw her like that," said her uncle. "I just want to believe that every human is a precious gem if the circumstances are right. But Saravette made her own circumstances. We tried to fix things, time after time. Time after time she wouldn't let us."

Death had come. They needed their pastor.

They got in Uncle Dean's car and drove to Chalk, where Miss Veola was waiting for them in the little yard under the big trees. They held each other and wept.

"I want the funeral to be private," said Lutie.

Miss Veola gave her a strange look.

"Nobody knows Saravette anymore," said Lutie.

"They know you, honey. Funeral's for you, too. You need to pray and sing and rejoice in the presence of the Lord and your friends."

"I still want it private," said Lutie.

"You just don't want them to know what kind of life Saravette led," said Miss Veola. "*I* don't want to know what life she led. *I* don't want to face the facts. *I* don't want proof that I failed one of my babies. Or that she failed me. You and I, we don't know which one it was. Only the Lord knows. But funerals—they're not about protecting our reputation. They're about sending the soul of somebody we loved to Jesus."

Aunt Tamika and Aunt Grace wept.

But I didn't love her, thought Lutie. I hardly knew her.

Lutie believed in heaven. She had never been able to close in on hell. But there had to be opposites. If the good people had eternal life in the presence of the Lord, then what about the bad people? Where did they go? Or were they all God's children in the end, folded in the arms of the Lord? Did he say, "It's okay. You're here now. Let's not worry about what happened then."

Lutie hoped not. Lutie hoped Saravette had to worry.

"I hurt too," said Miss Veola finally. "I hurt for my dear friend Eunice, who tried to be the best mama she knew how. Two out of three daughters turned out beautifully, and one was lost. But we have wept over that enough. Now is our time to give Saravette Painter food for her journey."

16

Azure Lee went to find Pierce. "Is it true your daddy showed up in school to yell at Train?"

"Yup," said Pierce glumly.

"This is not good," said Azure Lee. "Train knew perfectly well that you and I stopped that late bus because it was getting dark and Doria can be dumb as a stump and Train is not the person to hang with. Train probably already hates you. Why'd your daddy do that, anyway?"

"Evan at Youth Group said something about Train, and I thought it was my civic duty to call my daddy."

"You forgot what happened to Nate when he had that same idea?"

"I know, it was stupid."

"Watch yourself," said Azure Lee. Then she smiled. "Remember how Doria laughed at us the first time she heard us call our daddies *daddy*?"

"Yankees stop calling their daddies daddy when they're three. My daddy still calls *his* daddy daddy," said Pierce.

"You think there's any hope for Doria?"

"Well, you know, at Youth Group, I liked her. But she's hard to access. Like she's got some protective code."

"A firewall," agreed Azure Lee. "You want one in your computer, but you don't want one in your soul."

"Train has a bigger firewall. And I don't know if he even has a soul. He might be all firewall."

"When Train was little, he had perfect attendance pins for Sunday school."

"No way."

"True. He and Kelvin were going to be preachers."

"No way."

"True."

"I would rather pump septic tanks than be a preacher," said Pierce.

"It isn't your future that's the problem, Pierce. The problem is that Kelvin and Train are no longer cute little boys nobody can tell apart. These days, everybody loves Kelvin but nobody loves Train. No wonder he needs a firewall."

"The firewall is fine," said Pierce. "It's when Train decides to be the fire that worries me."

Death allowed a person to skip school. But Miss Veola did not allow a person to skip funeral planning.

Miss Veola was getting testy. "We need to decide what to sing, what scriptures to read, whether you girls want to talk about Saravette yourselves or whether you want me to do it all."

"Lutie must sing," said Aunt Tamika.

"No, thank you," said Lutie.

"It's your mama."

"She never sang to me."

"That has nothing to do with it," said Miss Veola. "She's going on her journey and—"

"And I never even knew her. She chose to be a stranger. And I am one. I have nothing to say or sing at her funeral."

"Lutie!"

"You're the ones who decided to tell me how my MeeMaw died, and who killed her. Should have kept it secret."

"Lutie, did you go to school today?"

"No."

"You'll go tomorrow."

"No."

"What's the matter with you, girl?"

Lutie stared at Miss Veola. What *wasn't* the matter?

⌒

The Music Appreciation class had already stomped into the music room when Mr. Gregg finally dismissed chorus. "Remember, next rehearsal we'll be singing shotgun!" he shouted.

"I'm next to Kelvin!" called at least five girls.

"I'm nice and wide," said Kelvin cheerfully. "Plenty of people can stand next to me." He swung his grin around the room. Then he saw Train and his grin faded.

Train had fixed him with those dead eyes. Kelvin had a terrifying sensation of being assessed as a victim.

The chorus headed for the door, but nobody could get out. Train and company filled the exit. They just stood there, slouched and silent.

"Singing shotgun?" repeated Train.

Nobody wanted to discuss the word "shotgun" with Train.

"I don't know what it means either," said Doria. "I barely know what a shotgun is. Let alone what it means to sing it."

"A shotgun scatters pellets," said one of the boys. "Normally a chorus sits in blocks. Soprano. Alto. Tenor. Bass. But next rehearsal we'll scatter, so nobody ends up sitting next to a person with the same part. Singing shotgun."

"Much richer sound," said Mr. Gregg, elbowing through the chorus. "Much better blend. Train, what's your problem? Don't stand in the door. People need to leave."

What isn't his problem? thought Kelvin.

Doria and Mr. Gregg shared the piano bench, working on Doria's latest composition.

"I've been working on the second act of my musical," said Mr. Gregg casually.

"How's it going?"

"Not good." Mr. Gregg tapped the piano keys with his pencil eraser. Tapped his wrist and then his chin. "I'm not sure I'm actually a composer."

Doria yearned for a good lie, an easy fib. Nothing came to mind.

Mr. Gregg sighed. "I've been kidding myself for a long time."

They sat for a while, absorbing this. Doria did not see how to soften the blow. "Will it leave a hole in your life to give up composing?" she asked finally. "Do you spend hours at it every week?"

"I carefully avoid it every week."

They laughed.

"You know what, Mr. Gregg? I want to quit my church job."

"No, don't. I always have a church job. Although I'm the choir director, not the organist. You get to present a different kind of music for a different reason and a different audience."

"So?" said Doria.

They laughed again.

"I also want to graduate this May, instead of next year."

Mr. Gregg studied her. "We've had kids graduate early. They come back and visit too often. I think they're sorry they threw away senior year. It's not like throwing away old sneakers, you know. You can't get another pair of senior years. Anyway, I know what you really want. You really want exactly what everybody else wants. You want girlfriends and a boyfriend."

The stab of truth went all the way through her chest and came out the other side.

He said, "You're panicking early. You've been here only two and a half months. Friendships will come."

"I'm not panicking," said Doria sharply.

"Skipping senior year isn't a sign of panic?"

"It's a sign of maturity and readiness."

"Dream on," said Mr. Gregg. "I, however, *am* mature. I'm admitting that I do not have a musical to show off to Professor Durham."

"On the other hand," said Doria, "he doesn't have the Laundry List to show off to you."

"And you do?"

"I have some of it. You know what, Mr. Gregg? My organ teacher thinks I need to coax Lutie to cooperate with the professor."

"That's exactly what I said! It's only meaningful if this organ teacher says it?"

"Sorry."

"And are you going to coax Lutie to share? Where is she this week, anyway? Sick or what?"

The funeral was this afternoon. *Don't talk about it,* Lutie had texted.

I won't, Doria texted back.

T, G and V want me to sing, Lutie texted.

Do it, Doria replied.

How disturbing that Mr. Gregg, who loved Lutie, did not know that Lutie's mother had died.

I'm not sure anybody else knows either, thought Doria. Nobody's talked about it. But maybe they're texting the news. Maybe everybody else has some new technology for communicating that nobody's even shown me. For all I know, the whole school's going to show up.

"I'll text her," said Doria, as if this answered Mr. Gregg's question.

The school day was over. Kids poured out the front doors.

Teams began to jog by, warming up for after-school practice. First came the singles: boys and girls completely into the physical demands of the run. Then the pairs: buddies who panted while they talked. Next the packs: groups who would slow down or speed up to stay together. Finally the laggards: kids who didn't care enough, had already run out of energy or were texting.

Again Kelvin found himself standing next to Train. Certainly he hadn't sought Train out. So Train had looked for him. The thought wasn't comforting.

Two boys ran by, perfect specimens of young manhood. They slowed down in front of an audience, showing off. What a contrast his thick body and Train's skinny body were. Kelvin briefly considered a diet.

"I could be on that team, if I wanted," said Train loudly.

Kelvin was an overweight slouch. Train was a rail-thin slouch. Neither one of them had any hope of being on any team. Except maybe as mascot. Kelvin entertained himself wondering who (besides DeRade) would want Train for a mascot. He had to laugh. Everybody joined in.

Train fixed his burning eyes on Kelvin.

Kelvin thought of the dead eye of poor Nate. He had never seen it. Nobody had. Nate's family moved away before Nate was even out of the hospital. And yet the eye haunted Kelvin.

He looked straight at Train, trying to find sweet little Cliff inside this person who had cut the barbed wire.

Not a trace.

He wants to do something, thought Kelvin. Actually, he has to do something. DeRade set the example. Train has to follow.

But Train was still at the stage where he needed an excuse. Even DeRade had needed an excuse—he couldn't blind a kid until the kid ratted on him.

Laughing at Train over football failure would not constitute an excuse to attack.

Or would it?

Normal behavior was burning off Train like pounds of flesh.

⟡

Train burned.

It wasn't enough that Kelvin had laughed at him.

Everybody had laughed.

Like they'd been hoping for a chance to laugh at him and Kelvin had given it to them.

DeRade—he used to think of stuff to do and then do it.

Train—he tagged along. Was that all he was good for? Since DeRade went to prison, Train hadn't done a thing except shuffle down the hallways, doing nothing.

That whole thing—stealing Doria's keys, taking her car,

making copies, letting himself into that church—had disgusted DeRade. *Loser,* he had texted.

Cell phones were illegal in prison, so of course everybody had one.

Doesn't get you into Slammer, DeRade texted.

Slammer was an Internet site that posted mug shots of people who had been arrested each week. Whether the accused had been booked for DUI or assault, bad checks or murder, Slammer published their photo online. If you wanted more information, you had to buy the weekly flyer at the convenience store.

All the wannabes did.

I'm a wannabe, thought Train, a little shocked.

Like he could peek at crime, but couldn't actually do it.

If he walked away now, the laughter would deepen and lengthen. DeRade would hear about it, because prison walls are not thick; they are porous. Everybody there knows everything.

Train felt as if his eyes had turned sideways, and now he was an animal that could not see straight ahead. He thought of DeRade in prison. No air, no sky, no wind, no grass. No girls. Endless jostling for power and space and safety. For years.

Train suddenly realized that he stood alone.

He was so boring to these kids that they had just drifted away.

People who were alone were nothing.

Train walked unsteadily to his locker. He was prepared. He had a bottle of rubbing alcohol, which they'd used on the kid on the TV news. He had a lighter. He had given the can lid thing a look—opened a huge can of peaches his mama had left in the cupboard and experimented using the lid as a knife. Cut his sandwich in quarters with it. But if he was going to cut somebody, he'd use an actual knife. Only he wasn't going to cut anyone.

He'd chosen fire.

He shut the locker door and his cell phone rang.

Miss Veola again.

Probably knew Pierce's daddy. Probably they had made plans together.

He would show them who made the plans.

Stop, she would have written.

If Miss Veola knew what he was going to do now, she would thunder, "The Lord God did his best for you! He gave his Son for you. Now you do your best for him, young man."

Train did not want to do his best. He wanted to do his worst.

Tuesday

Train chooses fire.
Doria chooses Cliff.
Lulie crosses the creek.
Kelvin sings shotgun.

17

Kelvin was puzzled by Miss Veola's message. It wasn't the usual *Stop*. It said, *Be sure to come.*

What did that mean? Come to what?

He walked slowly from the high school over to Tenth Street and turned north toward Miss Veola's.

Tenth Street was not lined with chain stores or strip malls. It had no traffic lights at this end. No employers. No schools. Streets sprouted here and there, hardly visible where they led into Chalk. The sidewalk switched from one side of the street to the other without warning. Here there was no pavement, just a thin trail worn into dry grass. Kelvin trudged up a small hill. From the top he would be able to see the pink church. It was oddly rural here. He was not thirty yards from Tenth Street, but it felt like he was on a farm.

Then suddenly out of the grass came Train.

Kelvin stopped.

Any remaining charm had been eaten off Train's face, as if by some interior monster. He looked starved. His eyes flared and his face widened as if something were hauling at his mouth.

He held a bottle of clear fluid in one hand and a cigarette lighter in the other.

Train smoked all the time. The lighter was no surprise. But what was he drinking?

Train unscrewed the cap of the bottle and Kelvin realized with horror that Train was not drinking out of it. It was for something else. He remembered the TV coverage from every night this week about that kid who'd been set on fire. That kid who'd lost seventy percent of his skin because of forty dollars he hadn't paid.

Train was ambushing him.

But Kelvin was one of the good guys. "Train?" he said.

Train laughed, high and vicious, like a hyena on a nature film.

Kelvin felt leaden.

He had to run, but he couldn't stand the thought of running. He saw himself ponderously, cravenly, lurching away from somebody half his weight—a kid who had been his friend in kindergarten! If Kelvin ran, only his back would get burned. Proof of cowardice.

Or proof of intelligence.

He said, "It's me, Train. Kelvin."

I can't be a victim, he thought.

"Victim." It meant a person killed as sacrifice, part of a rite. Train needed to shed blood, according to the ritual of DeRade.

Train's fingers were finding a position on the bottle when his cell phone rang.

Kelvin felt Train's desire to look at the phone. In that moment there was time to ponder the psychology of cell phones: how they always came first. You had to look. You had to know. Who wanted you?

That's everything, thought Kelvin. Who wants you? Nobody wants Train. Certainly I don't want Train.

Train couldn't ignore the ring. He looked, and his rhythm was broken. For an instant, his expression was normal. He was exasperated.

Kelvin made a guess. "Miss Veola?"

For one beat, Kelvin thought they were going to be okay. Train had been knocked off track in time to regain his sanity.

And then somebody else came up the hill and Train was an attack dog again.

Doria Bell. No street sense. No caution.

Doria would come right up here. Train might go for her instead. Doria, who would chat about Mozart as Train flicked his lighter.

Only his parents cared what happened to Kelvin. But Doria was a prize on any scale. Kelvin could not let Train hurt Doria.

∽

Doria was in a hurry.

She had brought good clothes to school and changed in the girls' room, but now her dressy shoes were slowing her down and she was mildly angry at her mother for refusing to let her drive the Honda today. She didn't want to walk fast enough to get sweaty, but if she dawdled she wouldn't have time to talk to Lutie before the service.

On the hill in front of her stood Kelvin and Train.

Their posture was out of tune. Their bodies were arched and stiff.

Doria often had the sensation of being all music. Now she had a new sensation. All fear.

It was thrilling and energizing. She wanted to run right

inside it. She wanted to hold it up like a glass window and smash through it.

Fear demanded speed.

"Hi, Cliff!" she yelled, racing up the hill. "Hi, Kelvin! Are you on your way to the funeral? Will you sit with me? I don't want to go alone."

Funeral? thought Kelvin.

Twenty feet away, Doria stopped. She bent over to adjust her black patent leather heels. She usually wore black, but this was not the vanishing black of her school clothes. Now she had on a black lace pencil skirt and a silky black tee. She was even wearing makeup.

Doria straightened. She looked beautiful and strange, like a magazine model stranded in the grass.

"What funeral?" said Train.

"Lutie's mother. You didn't hear? Her mother died on Sunday."

Kelvin and Train exchanged shocked glances.

Normal glances, thought Kelvin. Oh, God, can it be? Had Cliff just surfaced?

"Lutie's mother?" he said. He never thought of Lutie as having a mother. She had a grandmother. She had aunts.

"We should be at that funeral," said Kelvin to Train. "We're Lutie's friends."

Cliff Greene's fever ended, as if the thermometer had broken.

The terrible decision had been made.

He would not do it.

Not because of Miss Veola.

Not because of Doria Bell running up a hill.

Not even because of Lutie's sorrow.

228

The fever ended when Kelvin said "we." *We* should be at that funeral. *We're* Lutie's friends.

The terrible decision: go good or go bad.

Bad meant you always had followers.

Good meant you might have to go it alone. If he went good, he might be shunned and despised.

"The funeral is at Miss Veola's church," said Doria.

He would have to set foot in the house of the Lord.

I didn't blind Nate, he told the Lord. I stood there and let it happen, that's all.

So maybe I did blind Nate.

It was too terrible for forgiveness. The whole idea of forgiveness seemed as wrong as blinding Nate. He thought of Pierce's daddy telling him that being good was a ticket out.

Train did not want a ticket out. He wanted a ticket in.

He set the bottle of rubbing alcohol in the grass. He had shoplifted it new. Practiced with the half-finished bottle on the bathroom shelf. Worked fine. Exploded in flames.

"Rubbing alcohol?" asked Doria.

Kelvin said softly, "It's good for sore feet."

Doria frowned but didn't pursue it.

Kelvin said, "I don't think my parents know about Lutie's mother. I'd better call them. They'll want to be there. I can't believe I didn't know. What's her mother's name, anyway?"

"Saravette Painter. Isn't that a beautiful name? I'm not sure she was a beautiful person. Still. When your mother is dead, it has to be the beauty you think about. That would be your song. Miss Veola wants Lutie to sing from the Laundry List to honor her mother. Remember we heard her sing some of the songs the other day, Cliff?"

It was startling to hear his real name. To think that that person still existed. That he might still be Cliff Greene.

"I don't remember any songs about beauty," said Train. "But I know which one I'd choose."

☙

Train remembered hymns? Had favorites? Kelvin practically fell over.

Doria beamed as if they were about to climb onto an amusement park ride. She even clapped a little. Kelvin felt dizzy with the strangeness of this trio that he and Doria and Train formed.

"Sing it for me, Cliff," Doria begged.

She's the only person in Court Hill who calls him Cliff, thought Kelvin. Except Miss Veola and his mother. Maybe that's where we all went wrong. We let DeRade name him.

"I don't sing," said Cliff.

Although he did. Long ago and far away, they had been children in a Sunday-school choir, wearing silky robes and bright crosses hanging on ribbons.

Cliff scuffed the dirt with his huge filthy sneaker. "But for a funeral, I'd maybe choose 'Cross My Creek.'"

A minute ago, my life was in danger, thought Kelvin. Now Train is just another self-conscious boy facing a beautiful girl.

Kelvin gave Cliff a breather. He said to Doria, "The old Painter house is a half mile that way, across a creek. Didn't used to be a bridge. You had to go all the way around or wade. The Laundry List is different, you know. Those songs, they talk to the Lord different. Usually you invite people to come to the Lord, or you ask the Lord if *you* can go to *him*. But in 'Cross My Creek,' old Miz Painter tells the Lord to stop by. Set for a spell. Visit. And forgive each other's sins."

"Forgive *each other's* sins?" repeated Doria.

"'Cause the Lord was slow," said Cliff, as if he knew a

thing or two about the Lord being slow. "Old Miz Painter, she didn't think he should have been so slow." Cliff took a big breath, then looked down, as if he really were on a cliff. Teetering.

He wants to sing, thought Kelvin. That's why he took Music Appreciation. Not to ruin Mr. Gregg's life. He wants to sing.

"How does it go?" asked Doria. "'Cross My Creek'?"

Cliff took another breath.

Kelvin prayed.

Cliff sang.

Cross my creek, Mabel Painter had ordered the Lord. And then the melody softened. *I'll wash your feet, Lord*, she offered. And then, like giving him a present—*and you wash mine.*

The song rolled on, telling the Lord to set for a spell, and not fret for a spell.

"Oh, Cliff!" said Doria. "Your voice is so warm and sweet." She was certainly the only person in Court Hill to describe Train with those words. "I can just see you on the far side of the creek, beckoning to the Lord as if he's the shy one and you have to let him know he's welcome."

Cliff was embarrassed. "Miz Painter would have had a basin," he told her, without meeting her eyes, "Like my grandmother's. White stuff on metal. What's it called, Kelvin?"

"Enamel. We got one too."

"Anyway, she didn't have running water. She'da sat in her rocker on the front porch and washed her feet before she went inside, to get that red dirt off them."

"She did laundry and didn't have running water?" Doria was incredulous. She said, "Cliff, you know how people speak up at funerals and offer little stories about the dead person? We didn't know Lutie's mother, so we can't tell some cool story about her. But you can stand up and sing. You don't need a piano any more than Mabel Painter did or Lutie does. I think those words belong at the beginning of the funeral service. You invite everybody in. 'Cross my creek,' you'll say to them."

Cliff stared at her in astonishment. "Not me."

Kelvin said, "Anyway, we're not dressed for a funeral."

Cliff looked down at his torn purple T-shirt, his soiled baggy jeans and his filthy sneakers with laces trailing in the dust.

All his life, Kelvin would remember the moment in which the baddest kid in school knelt to tie his shoelaces, the closest he could get to dressing formal for a funeral.

Kelvin called his mother on his cell phone.

"Saravette?" she cried. "Oh, Kelvin! I thought she was dead long ago! I am shocked. I should be there! When is it? I don't think I can get there in time!"

"You knew her?" Kelvin felt hurt. His parents knew he adored Lutie and they'd never mentioned that she had a mother somewhere out there?

"Of course I knew her. Lutie looks just like her. Saravette and her mama fought every minute of every day her whole life. Saravette disappeared years ago. I just had no idea that—well— I'm hurrying. You go comfort Miss Lutie for me, Kelvin."

What a great idea.

He and Cliff were down the hill now, where the sidewalk started up again. Miss Veola's church was just down the road. A long white funeral-home limo was just pulling up. Kelvin placed a mental bet on whether Cliff would actually enter the church. Whether he could hang on to being Cliff, or whether Train would be back on track in a minute.

A crowd milled around the pink church.

A little too far for Kelvin to recognize anybody, but Cliff stopped short, like a foot smashing the brake.

232

He sees somebody he knows, thought Kelvin. He's Train again. He's got an image to preserve. He's not going into that pink church. Not now. Not ever. But at least I haven't been burned over seventy percent of my body.

Train looked over his shoulder, so Kelvin did too.

Doria was framed against the sky at the top of the hill. She had not followed.

I prayed for the wrong thing, thought Kelvin.

Cliff Greene walked back up the hill. "Yeah. Sit with us," he said.

The church was filling up.

No matter what Lutie and her aunts half wished, funerals are not private.

Friends come. It is their job to offer comfort. To cry with you, sing with you and pray with you. To bring casseroles and desserts. To tell stories of good times. To laugh.

There were no good times to share in Saravette's life.

No funny moments.

All the stories were sad.

Who had she been? A woman who'd tossed her life in the gutter and never bothered with the fine things she could have had: family and love and a daughter.

Lutie was glad she had left that greasy little diner so fast. The fewer memories she had of Saravette, killer of MeeMaw, the better. She could not stand it if Miss Veola got all senti-mental and Christian about Saravette. Let God forgive Sar-avette's sins, if he had that much time.

Lutie paced, ignoring the choir robe shot through with gold threads that Miss Veola had laid out, hoping Lutie would sing. She accepted a hug here and words of condolence there.

The professor walked in.

His jaw dropped, like everybody's the first time they saw

Miss Veola's paint job, and he smothered an incredulous laugh, just like everybody. It was a good way to start a Sunday, laughing in pink. But this wasn't Sunday.

Martin Durham was not here as a friend of the family. He could have come for one reason only: a crack at the Laundry List. Sure enough, he chose a back pew, where he sat like a tourist, checking out women's hats and the altar flowers.

Then through the door of the pink church walked Kelvin and Train, with Doria between them. Kelvin and Train looked sweaty and dirty. Doria looked elegant and shimmery. They were a startling trio.

Doria and Kelvin sat down in a pew. And then, to Lutie's horror, Train walked up the aisle to the chancel. He swayed. There was fear on his face. His posture and his gait were all wrong.

Fear shot through Lutie.

What was Train planning? Even the police had known he was planning something.

A mass murder, where a crazed shooter killed an entire congregation?

Miss Veola was as stricken as Lutie. She put herself between Train and Lutie, as if to take the bullet.

Train whispered, "Can I sing 'Cross My Creek'?"

Jesus stepped on Lutie Painter's toes.

Or maybe it was Cliff.

For the first time in her life, she understood the old hymn about the ninety and nine, where Jesus left the flock of sheep on its own and went off into the dark and the storm to find the lost one.

Lutie had not bothered to find the lost one.

Couldn't care less about the lost one.

Had even sat in a diner with the lost Saravette, but said nothing, offered nothing, did nothing—and walked out.

And the same with Cliff Greene. When he began to tilt wrong, and run wrong, and enjoy wrong, not once had Lutie Painter headed into the dark for his sake.

I'm the sinner, she thought. Not Saravette.

I'm a fake. Posturing, boasting, telling everybody how special I am. Nodding in agreement when everybody says, *What a great voice! What a great mind! Of course she's in AP classes. Of course she sings solos.* Special Lutie.

While all along, I've been one of the comfortable ones. One of the safe ones.

Oh, sure, you can sing about sin and cleansing your heart, but you never think *you* committed any sins; it's people in the audience who committed the sins.

And then Jesus steps on your toes.

Miss Veola, in her white robe with its white sash, put her arms around Train's thin sweaty dirty self. "I prayed for this," she said softly. "I've always prayed for you, Cliff. You were always furious with me for it. Have you forgiven me?"

"I'm not a good person," whispered Train.

"Then you've chosen the very best song at the very best time," said Miss Veola, letting go of him. She held her arms out wide, bringing her whole congregation into her embrace. She raised her voice. "Cliff Greene will welcome us with a song called 'Cross My Creek.' Some of us know it already. It's easy to learn. Cliff will get us started, and then we'll all come in."

The older people in the room began to cry.

Because they knew "Cross My Creek"? Because they remembered Eunice Painter singing it?

Or because a lost child had come home?

In the back of the church, the professor took a thin gleaming state-of-the-art-looking device from his briefcase.

Cliff Greene was paralyzed. It had happened to him before. It had happened when DeRade actually got to work on Nate. He had stood there, getting cold, staring.

Now he stood cold and staring at the congregation. He was horrified by having an audience. He knew that they must be equally horrified by him.

I did a lot wrong, he thought. A lot of times. I did it to impress DeRade. But that's no excuse. And now I'm hoping for a ticket in, but I haven't done anything to deserve it. I didn't become a good person. I just didn't become a worse person.

He couldn't get any air.

He couldn't remember how to start anything—a life, a breath or a song.

The congregation was leaning toward him, willing him to come in. Doria kept breathing deep, as if teaching the subject. Kelvin just looked pleased with life, his big sloppy grin waiting for the next act.

If this is just an act, thought Cliff, it's nothing.

I have to do it right. Can't just be words. I gotta call to the Lord.

He could still walk out. He could still laugh at these people.

Kelvin straightened up. He made a lifting gesture with both hands, a sort of rolling of his palms. It said, *Come on. You can do it.*

⟳

Doria felt Cliff's nervousness slip toward terror.

Standing on that step, facing the crowd, wearing the wrong clothes—clothes matter when you have an audience—Cliff looked as if he would not make it.

In her experience, terror helped a performance. You pulled

yourself over it and through it, and it strengthened you. She nodded at him. *You can do it,* she told him.

He stared at her as one stares at a piece of meaningless modern art.

Doria took a deep breath to remind him how it was done. He didn't pull in enough air for one note, let alone a song.

He breathed a second time, and a third, and now the whole church was praying for him, breathing deep and offering air, and finally he began to sing.

> *"Cross my creek.*
> *Cross my creek, Lord.*
> *I'll wash your feet, Lord.*
> *And you wash mine."*

When he had circled the song twice, Miss Veola joined in, and then Lutie, and then the whole room.

They gave Cliff a standing ovation, and Doria felt as if a lot more was happening than a stranger could tell. She raised her eyebrows at Kelvin. "They're clapping him home," Kelvin whispered.

She and Kelvin shifted down the pew so Cliff could fit back in.

"Good job," she whispered.

⟳

It was the first time in years that Cliff Greene had wanted to do a good job.

First time in years he wanted to act in the light instead of the dark.

He prayed his mother would take him back.

He prayed for his brother.

An arm went around his shoulder. Kelvin's arm was heavy. The weight of it pressed Cliff into the pew and felt good.

⟳

"We are here," said Miss Veola, "to remember the life of Saravette Painter. She suffered. She did many things wrong and few things right. But she was loved. She was loved especially by her mother, Eunice Painter, who never—not even at the last moment of her life—stopped loving her little girl. Now Saravette has crossed the most important creek. She will wash the feet of the Lord and he will wash hers."

Half the room was sobbing. Lutie thought, Do they know? Was it not a secret after all? Do these elderly ladies in their shiny hats know how my MeeMaw died?

"Let us pray," said the pastor. "Lord, we thank you for everyone in this room. We thank you for the courage of Cliff Greene. We thank you for friendship and music and neighbors."

Lutie was not sitting where she belonged, with her aunts and other relatives in the front. She was still in the chancel. She had lowered herself into a deacon's chair when Cliff began to sing.

A metallic shimmer caught her eye and she looked up.

One head was not bowed. The professor was looking around, mildly interested, somewhat amused. In one hand he held what she assumed was a recording device, or maybe just a really good phone.

Lutie thought, He really does need the Laundry List. Even here, even now, he doesn't feel God or love or the pain of life. He's just working on his career.

Lutie pitied him with all her heart. How nice that she still had all her heart. She hadn't destroyed it when she wanted her own mother never to show up.

"Lord, have mercy on your children," said Miss Veola, "especially the ones who did a bad job with life. Love all of us anyway. Take your daughter Saravette in your arms and welcome her to heaven. And your sons and daughters here on earth, Lord, help them use their lives for something beautiful. Something brave. Don't let them fritter away their lives."

Lutie felt the strong women from whom she had descended climbing through the years and into her heart. She felt their songs and voices rising.

She became aware that the church was very quiet. This was not a group that worshipped in silence. What was the matter?

Miss Veola had sat down.

The people waited.

It was time.

Lutie stood. She walked forward. She placed her feet where Cliff had stood.

"I'm going to sing the only song on the Laundry List that's actually about laundry," she told the congregation. "I hardly ever sing this one. Mabel Painter, my grandmother's grandmother, wanted a grand life and she didn't get one. My MeeMaw liked to tell me that Mabel Painter's prayers came true, but not for her. Her prayers came true for me."

Lutie found herself with even less air than Cliff had had. Her next breath still barely held her body up. This is how tired Mabel Painter was, every day of her life, thought Lutie. But she went on. And so will I.

From the back, in the silence, came a little click.

Uncle Dean quietly left the first pew and walked to the rear. Lutie forgot sometimes that her uncle had played football; in fact, he had had a football scholarship. His shoulders were wider than most men's.

Uncle Dean stepped over a few legs, and squashed into the pew next to Martin Durham.

The professor looked like a child next to Uncle Dean.

They had a short chat.

Uncle Dean took custody of the recorder.

Lutie said, "Saravette was my mother. She made bad choices. I made a bad choice too. I never wanted to find her. She got lost, she stayed lost, and I was glad. I stayed with the ninety and nine, and we were all safe and clean and had houses with granite countertops and central air."

Lutie's confession stabbed Kelvin in the heart.

He wanted to run up the aisle and hug her forever and squash the guilt out of her. Lutie wasn't responsible for Saravette!

Lutie struggled for breath, like the basketball player whose last free throw will win or lose the championship. She blew out one long huff of air to calm herself. She said, "Saravette never heard me sing. This is my last chance."

Lutie raised one hand.

Sometimes when she sang hands up, she was conducting herself, adding more beat. Sometimes she was waving. "Hey, Lord. You like your song?" Mostly she was signaling that she was a believer. This time, she was cupping the good news in her palm and pulling it in.

> *"Ain't got no sword,*
> *Got just an ironing board.*
> *Can't fight for you, Lord.*
> *But show me where to stand, Lord.*
> *Want to make life here grand, Lord."*

Saravette had not had anything grand on earth, nor had she tried to make anything grand.

But she's with the Lord now, thought Lutie. That's pretty grand.

> *"Lord, I done give all I got to give.*
> *Don't have to iron up where you live.*
> *I'm too tired to stand, Lord.*
> *Don't care if life's grand, Lord."*

Lutie was in the home stretch. Only the refrain was left. She stopped and wiped away tears and pulled herself together. And then she finished Saravette's song.

> *"Take me home, Lord.*
> *Take me home."*

18

So much food.

Biscuits and barbecue, salads and chicken, casseroles and pie.

Piles of white paper napkins and red plastic plates.

Jugs of tea and lemonade. Pitchers of coffee.

Aunt Tamika and Aunt Grace welcomed everybody to the reception in the church hall, hugging and exclaiming and hugging again.

In walked Lieutenant Andrews and his son, Pierce.

"Donny!" cried Aunt Tamika. "You came! You're such a sweetheart." She kissed him.

Lutie almost fell over. Aunt Tamika knew this cop? Liked him?

Her aunt said, "Lutie, honey, do you know Pierce's daddy? Donny Andrews is the one could always find Saravette when nobody else could."

Miss Veola said, "Mika, you keeping Donny to yourself? Hey, Donny."

"Miss Veola," said Pierce's father, smiling. "I didn't get here in time for the funeral. I'm sorry about that. And I'm sorry I didn't get there in time to find your sister, Mika. We tried. When you called, we went hunting, but I guess we hit the wrong places."

Aunt Tamika said, "Donny and I were in high school together. Cochaired a dance once. Acted in a play. Three years of math in the same section."

Lutie felt this information should have been passed on years ago.

"Hi, Lutie," said Pierce. "I didn't know any of that either. My daddy never tells stuff invades anybody's privacy."

What privacy was Pierce talking about? And then Lutie realized: her own. Pierce's daddy had probably always known that Lutie was the daughter of that sorry case. And he'd never once told.

"I'm sorry about your loss," Pierce said formally. He handed over a plastic cake holder, with a strap over the high lid, which a church lady swept away and carried over to the dessert table.

"Your mother baked a cake?" said Lutie. Had Pierce's mother gone to high school with Aunt Tamika as well and Lutie hadn't known that, either?

"We couldn't come empty," said Pierce. "Hey, Kelvin. Hey, Doria." He shot a glance at his father and then said nervously, "Hey, Train."

"It's too bad you missed the service," said Doria. "Of course you knew that Lutie would sing and be fabulous, but guess what? Cliff sang, and he was fabulous."

Pierce's mouth fell open.

Lutie knew the feeling.

Miss Elminah was handing them dessert plates with generous slices of Pierce's mother's cake, and red plastic forks.

"I love dessert first," said Kelvin. There was his mama coming in, all of a flurry because she'd missed the service and didn't have any food with her. But she was here.

243

"Your mom looks pretty," said Cliff.

"Tell her that," said Kelvin. "Nothing she likes more than a man telling her she's pretty." Kelvin thought of an old hymn: *Order my steps, Lord. I want to walk worthy.*

Had Cliff Greene wanted to walk worthy all along and couldn't? Because his brother and his neighbors were nailing him to a track that went the other direction?

And when did I ever step up, Kelvin asked himself, and pull him back?

Kelvin liked to think of himself as one who walked worthy. But he hadn't taken one step toward Cliff, and time after time, he had walked away from Train.

Cliff had to get here alone, thought Kelvin.

Miss Veola bustled up. How small she was. Like a chipmunk compared to Kelvin. She said, "I have prayed so long, Cliff Greene, that it wore ruts in my prayers. And here you are."

The high emotion that had brought Train to the altar to sing was back under control. He shrugged. "Maybe."

Miss Veola began to pray and both boys scrunched down, hoping she would lower her voice and that it would end soon, but that was never the case with Veola Mixton and the Lord.

Lutie saw Mr. Gregg charge in the door. He stopped, squinted and looked around for people he knew. He greeted Miss Veola and then Lutie's aunts, whom he knew from concerts, and finally Lutie. "You sang from the Laundry List and I wasn't here?" he accused her. "Lutie!"

"This was her mother's funeral, Mr. Gregg," Doria reminded him.

"Oh, right. I wasn't thinking. I'm so sorry for your loss, Lutie. How are you managing?"

"Fine, thanks, Mr. Gregg. Thank you for coming."

"Did anybody record it? Can I hear it? Can you do it again for me?" he asked.

There was something wonderful about his single-mindedness. Lutie loved him. "We haven't recorded any of the songs, Mr. Gregg. But we will. I'm thinking that my uncle Dean and my aunts and I will go to a lawyer first. And then you and Professor Durham and all of us will decide what's next."

"I get to be in on it? Think my name could appear on the CD? I am, like, so dying for worldwide attention."

Lutie was laughing. "It's more likely to be Court Hill–wide than worldwide."

"Nope. National treasure," he said.

"You haven't even heard any of the songs yet," she pointed out.

Mr. Gregg swung on Doria. "Doria," he demanded. "Those songs national treasure or mediocrity?"

"Treasure," said Doria, smiling. "But maybe not national. Maybe the personal property of the Painter family."

"Wait, wait, wait," said Miss Veola. "If Jimmy Gregg gets to be on the CD, do I get my benefit performance? I have a church to build, you remember."

Lutie was suddenly awash in tears. It was her church being built bigger and finer. And she almost hadn't helped. "What's a good date?"

⟋

"Let us give thanks!" called Miss Veola.

People who had been eating all along pretended they hadn't.

Silence slowly settled on the room.

Heads bowed. Even Cliff Greene's. He stared down at his plastic plate. It was covered with chocolate crumbs and a slick of icing. Miss Veola launched into a blessing over the food,

245

and Cliff stood on the outside of the prayer. These people had easy lives and an easy tomorrow. But when he went back to school, contempt would replace respect on many faces. He could already feel the shame of backing down. What Miss Veola called victory, everybody Cliff knew would call defeat.

Could he do this? Stay on this side of life?

Did he want to?

He closed his eyes and let his own words roll back. *Cross my creek, Lord. Wash my feet, Lord. And I'll wash yours.*

It worked, a little.

But it didn't work enough. He wanted out. He didn't want one more old lady touching him or smiling at him. He didn't want these easy safe people who had so much to be thankful for.

Outside Fellowship Hall was air and safety.

Outside he could be Train.

He turned away, letting Cliff fall off like a jacket.

Kelvin watched him go.

In school tomorrow, thought Kelvin, in front of all the guys he wants to impress, and all the guys he *has* impressed, and all the guys DeRade assigned him—it won't be easy to be Cliff. Being Train—that would be easy. We need to sing shotgun with Cliff, one of us on each side, so he can't end up next to the usual voice part.

Nice plan. One flaw. Cliff had to cooperate.

"Amen!" called Miss Veola.

I'm not great at school and I don't care, thought Kelvin. I'm not great at sports and I don't care. I'm great at one thing, though, and I do care about that.

Lord, he said silently, you and me got to work together here. Gotta keep Cliff from being Train long enough for it to stick.

Voices and laughter filled the room, and the crowd looked for Lutie and her aunts, and people filled their plates, and Kelvin caught up to Cliff and filled the exit. "Let's fix a plate to take to your mama," he said. "When we bring it by, I'm going to tell her all about the funeral. She'll want to know how great you sang."

Kelvin didn't see his kindergarten friend in the silent person standing beside him. But he didn't see DeRade, either. I can do this, Kelvin told himself. I can guide some steps. "Besides, I wanna talk," he said to Cliff. "You won't believe what I'm thinking. *I* can't believe what I'm thinking."

Cliff didn't show any interest but he didn't reach for the doorknob either.

"I'm thinking I might be a preacher after all," said Kelvin.

"Well, don't make it sound like throwing yourself in front of a bus," said Cliff.

"I can't go it alone," said Kelvin.

"You have me join, you're gonna have a awful small crowd. Nobody else would come."

"Two's a start, though. But you know what? First? Let's eat. You check out that dessert table? It's awesome." Kelvin bumped Cliff back into the room. Toward the good food. And the good people.

◌

Trees clap hands and sing, thought Veola Mixton. There are blessings all around.

She watched her young people. To her they were all young.

She decided not to text the word "Stop" anymore.

She would write *Go*.

Go with the Lord. Go with each other.

Go.

◌

247

Azure Lee and Doria had finished Pierce's mama's cake and were looking over the biscuit selection. Ham biscuits, chicken biscuits, biscuits with gravy. Azure Lee bit down thoughtfully into a ham biscuit. "Pierce likes you," she said.

"Seriously?"

"Yup."

"How do you know?"

"He said."

"Clearly?"

"Clear enough. Go over there and talk to him, Doria. It's perfectly reasonable, you know. You're the only white kids here."

Doria whispered, "I have this crush on Kelvin."

"Everybody has a crush on Kelvin. Give it up. Go talk to Pierce."

Doria looked over. Pierce was looking her way already. Smiling at her. He held out a plate, like he wanted to share the dessert that lay on it. She began walking toward him just as her cell phone rang. It was Nell's ringtone. Doria turned her phone off. "Hi, Pierce. Your mama made a great cake."

"My *mama*?" he repeated, laughing. "Next thing you're going to ask to meet my *daddy*."

"I might even call him sir."

"No way. You gotta stay a little bit Yankee. That's half the fun."

Half the fun, thought Doria, would be twice the fun I usually have.

Pierce put two more desserts on her plate.

Across the table, Kelvin rescued Cliff's dessert plate just in time. Lutie flung her arms around Cliff and said, "Oh, you were the best. Thank you for singing. It made me cry. It made me know things. It made me feel good."

Music, thought Doria. And prayer. And friends. They do that.

AUTHOR'S NOTE

I've always gone to church, but beginning in my early teens, I didn't sit in the pew with everybody else. I was the organist. I had my first church job two years before I was old enough to drive. When I was in junior high and high school, I accompanied my school choirs, and when I had my own family, I accompanied all their school choruses.

A few years ago, I moved from Connecticut to South Carolina. Choosing a church was difficult. I attended several, from a tiny country church to a megachurch. When I finally found the church that was just right for me, I decided to sing in the choir instead of play the organ.

One Sunday, there was a request in the bulletin for volunteers the next Saturday afternoon. I signed up. It was a hot-meal ministry in a community called Paradise. "Paradise" to me is a word reserved for the heaven that Jesus promised to the thief on the cross beside him.

It was so strange to use it in ordinary conversation. "I'll be serving supper in Paradise." "Have you been to Paradise yet?" "What did you think of Paradise?" I have seldom had a Saturday afternoon that provided more food for thought.

But Paradise did not seem quite the right name for this neighborhood. I asked several people where the name came from. Everybody agreed that the name Paradise had been given to the community because generations ago, women there had taken in laundry, and they sang as they worked, and when people drove in to pick up their laundry, the singing sounded like paradise. I loved that story. I never verified it. I just went home and started to write. What had those women been singing? What songs had kept them going over the years and through the labor?

I wrote the songs in this book so easily that I felt as if I had been singing them all along. And perhaps I had. I think the yearning for God to come in person and help in time of trouble is universal. And I strongly believe that another yearning in each of us is the desire to help others. There's nothing as satisfying as lending a hand. I loved writing this book, and I loved all the people, and the songs they sang, and the help they gave.

ACKNOWLEDGMENTS

I thank Mary Baker; her husband, Jimmy; and their son, young Jimmy, for serving supper in Paradise, and letting me be part of it. I thank Sherry Boyce, who suggested that I should sign up for it, and who was an early reader of this manuscript and corrected several errors. I thank the people of Paradise Community. Thanks to young-adult librarian Cheryl Brown, who read the manuscript and whose comments were so encouraging. Thanks to our minister, John Warren, whose sermon I am quoting and whose name I am using. Thanks to Fort Mill, the town in which I live, where I am constantly awed by yet another person who is generous with time, money, work and prayer.

Most of all I thank Beverly Horowitz, my editor, who kept me going as I floundered through many variations on a theme and who helped me to reach the story I wanted to tell.

ABOUT THE AUTHOR

Caroline B. Cooney is the author of many books for young people, including *Three Black Swans; They Never Came Back; If the Witness Lied; Diamonds in the Shadow; A Friend at Midnight; Hit the Road; Code Orange; The Girl Who Invented Romance; Family Reunion; Goddess of Yesterday* (an ALA-ALSC Notable Children's Book); *The Ransom of Mercy Carter; Tune In Anytime; Burning Up; The Face on the Milk Carton* (an IRA-CBC Children's Choice Book) and its companions, *Whatever Happened to Janie?* and *The Voice on the Radio* (each of them an ALA-YALSA Best Book for Young Adults), as well as *What Janie Found; What Child Is This?* (an ALA-YALSA Best Book for Young Adults); *Driver's Ed* (an ALA-YALSA Best Book for Young Adults and a *Booklist* Editors' Choice); *Among Friends; Twenty Pageants Later;* and the Time Travel Quartet: *Both Sides of Time, Out of Time, Prisoner of Time,* and *For All Time,* which are also available as *The Time Travelers,* Volumes I and II.

Caroline B. Cooney lives in South Carolina.